RANGER

Book 1:

A Humble Beginning

By Darrell Maloney

This book is dedicated to my brother, Randy Maloney, who
passed away a few months ago.

Randy was strong and forthright, like the character in this
book who shares his name.

He was also one of the finest men I've ever known. I miss
him and love him so very much.

You'd have loved him too.

Randy, this is for you.

For the latest information about this book and the author's other
works, please visit
darrellmaloney.com

Chapter 1

He was born Randall, but came to hate the name. As a youngster, he implored his friends to call him Randy. Randy had a certain zing to it, he said. A certain flair. To him, Randall was just the sissified version. It was a name assigned with one who wore fancy clothing and drank hot tea.

Randy hated hot tea.

When he grew a little older he took to writing Randy on his school papers, and on those rare "official" forms he had to fill out. An application to join the Cub Scouts. Another form to mark his advance to the Webelos, and yet another when he became a Boy Scout.

After awhile, he pretty much forgot he even had a formal given name, despite his Grandma Maloney's insistence on calling him Randall at all family gatherings. And to the other little old ladies at the family's church who always pinched his cheeks and told him how cute he was.

It wasn't until he had the application for the Texas Rangers in front of him that he finally faced a major dilemma regarding the name. And he wasn't sure what to do.

To most people it seemed such a simple thing. To most people a name was a name was a name.

But Randy wasn't like most people. The name issue was a big thing to him. A major thing, in fact.

He had a choice.

The form said, in Block 1, "Given Name."

Try as he might, he couldn't see any wiggle room. No way to legally fail to complete the block as requested and still, with good conscience, sign the bottom of the form.

In Block 34.

The one that said, "Under penalty of perjury I attest that all information on this form is true and correct to the best of my knowledge."

He couldn't start his career in the premier law enforcement agency of the Great State of Texas under the cloud of a lie.

In fact, Randy seldom lied at all. Others lied at the drop of a hat, but Randy could count on one hand the number of times he'd ever told one. He felt that bad about each one. The last one, when he told a girlfriend she was beautiful when she looked like a ran-over possum with a hangover, was over three years before.

He didn't like to lie.

But he didn't want anyone at the Ranger School, or in the ranks after he won his five-pointed star, to call him Randall.

He shuddered at the thought of his training instructors finding out he hated the name, and using it every chance they got to try to make him lose his cool.

For two full minutes he looked at the form, debating which way to go.

The administrative specialist on the other side of the counter grew concerned.

"Is your pen out of ink, sir? I can get you another one."

"Huh? Oh… no. It's fine."

The clerk's brother was afflicted with a form of epilepsy, and suffered from frequent "blank moments" when he would freeze and stare out into space for a minute or two.

She was convinced that this strapping young man standing at the counter was afflicted with the same ailment, and that the stress of filling out the form had sent him into a blank moment.

She pitied him, for she knew that such an ailment would disqualify him during the mandatory physical examination later in the process.

But she wasn't going to tell him that. She didn't have the heart to.

She watched him as he suddenly began to write, sure that his blank moment had ended and that he was back among the rest of them, now conscious of his surroundings again.

She wasn't too far off the mark, for Randy had indeed snapped out of the sorry state he'd been in. But it had nothing at all to do with epilepsy or blank moments.

It had everything to do with the epiphany Randy had. A solution to his problem. The answer to his dilemma.

Luckily, Block 1 was fairly good sized. And Randy could write fairly small when he printed in block letters. And it helped that the administrative clerk had the forethought to give him a fine-tip pen.

He stuck his tongue out the side of his mouth as he wrote. He always did that when he focused on something. His mom thought it was cute and told him so. He tried his best over the years to stop doing it, until he discovered that other women thought it cute as well. Then he learned to embrace it.

In small letters in Block 1 he answered the question, and then some.

"Randall (But I go by Randy please)."

That should do it.

Only it didn't.

What it did do was open a door for the instructors at the Texas Ranger Academy. They reviewed his application after he was accepted into the training program. And they decided to find out exactly how sensitive he was to his formal first name.

"Get your ass out of bed, *Randall*," they'd yell at the top of their lungs. "You're wasting my time, *Randall*. You should have been dressed ten minutes ago, *Randall*. And what's with those shoes? What happened to the shine? Did you shine those shoes with a Hershey bar, *Randall*?"

He took it all in stride. He had no choice. And after the first three weeks of the twelve week course, they laid off a bit.

The Texas Ranger Academy wasn't very different from Marine Corps boot camp. One of the primary jobs of the training instructors was to try to break the men down into quivering puddles of jelly. The thinking was, if they couldn't take being yelled at, if they couldn't take being insulted and chided and ridiculed in a controlled situation… then they couldn't stand the rigors of real life police work.

It was a system which worked quite well for over a hundred years, both for military induction sites and for the Texas Rangers. Those who were weak were weeded out. Those who were strong enough to complete the training grew stronger from it.

And for Randy, the whole name issue was minor in the grand scheme of things.

He excelled in every facet of his training. The highest possible scores on the written tests as well as his personnel evaluations. The first to finish the daily four mile run, and the only man in the unit who went back to run beside the laggers.

To encourage them not to give up.

Giving up was not something Randy ever did. Or tolerated from his friends.

Randy graduated at the top of his class from the Ranger Academy.

His father, a retired Ranger himself, accepted an invitation from the Academy's commandant to be present for Randy's graduation.

And to pin on his son's first badge.

Randy only wore his shiny new badge for one day, as was the minimum stated in the Ranger's handbook.

After that, he was given permission to replace it with a similar badge once worn by his great great grandfather, Wilford P. Maloney.

For Randy wasn't the first Texas Ranger in the family. Old Wilford P. had started the tradition back in 1895 when West Texas was still inhabited by bands of hostile Indians. He lied about his age and joined the Rangers at age fifteen. That was said to be the only lie he'd ever told.

They jokingly called it the "family business," the Maloneys did. Randy was the fifth Maloney in five successive generations to wear old Wilford P.'s badge.

It was a bit more dented and tarnished than the day Wilford P. first pinned it on.

But it had the same symbolism.

Chapter 2

Randy's early days in the Rangers were easy ones. He was assigned to a training officer who was a very likeable guy. The life of the proverbial party, the class clown and the go-to guy all rolled up into one package.

"Stick to Ranger Wagner like glue," his lieutenant told him. "He's the best we've got. He'll show you everything you need to know."

And he did. After his ninety day probation period was up, Randy was called in to take a series of practical evaluations.

They weren't yes or no questions. No multiple choice either. They were scenarios, laid out in detail, for which there were several possible solutions.

But only one that the evaluators considered ideal.

There were two other probationers in the room with Randy, taking the same tests.

Randy was the only one who passed. And he passed by such a large margin that one of the evaluators did something totally unprecedented.

He found Randy before he left the building and shook his hand.

"You'll make a fine Ranger, Maloney. You can think on your feet. That's a quality that's getting harder and harder to find. You'll do well in your family business."

Word had gotten around that Randy was fifth generation Ranger, and was proud of it. He was frequently asked about his badge, and why it was nicked and worn when other rookie Rangers' badges were shiny and new.

He'd always taken great pride in explaining how Wilford P. had worn the very same badge into battle. First against the Comanche and then against rustlers and killers and the worst that mankind had to offer. His great grandfather took the badge from Wilfred P. when the elder was forced to retire at ten years. It was Ranger policy back then, for the Rangers figured that any man who'd served ten years and survived was living on borrowed time.

Wilford P. fought hard to stay, but the powers that be overruled him and forced him out to pasture.

Randy's dad told him it was the only fight Wilford P. ever lost.

Randy did indeed have a family legacy to live up to.

And it didn't take long for him to have the chance to show his mettle.

The very next day after he blew the evaluators away with his test scores... his first day off of probation and as a full-fledged Ranger, he saw something.

His partner, Wagner, was at the wheel of a car leaving downtown Austin. The pair was headed to San Saba to do the preliminary groundwork on a new investigation. It was alleged that the sheriff of San Saba County was bought and paid for by a local real estate developer. And that he was doing everything in his power to squeeze the developer's competition out of the county.

As they cruised down Capitol Avenue on their way to Interstate 35, Randy saw a glint of light inside a local bank.

It wasn't much. Just a quick flash reflected off of something in a man's hand as he entered the building.

And in reality, it could have been anything. A silver cell phone reflecting the light from an overhead fluorescent bulb. A silver ink pen held by a man getting ready to endorse a check. A silver bracelet.

But Randy had a hunch. And his father told him never to ignore a hunch. Sometimes they played out, sometimes they didn't. But to ignore a hunch was to miss an opportunity. And frequently that opportunity was the only one a Ranger got.

"Tony, pull around the corner and let me out, will you?"

"What's up, Randy? What ya got?"

"I don't know. Probably nothing. Just drop me off and circle the block a few times. There may be something going on in the First Union Bank."

It turned out that his partner was a big believer in hunches as well. No more words were necessary. Wagner turned the corner and stopped the car just long enough to let Randy out. Then he raced up the block and grabbed the first available parking space before exiting the car himself and following fifty yards behind his partner.

Randy walked into the bank and took his place in line behind a woman of about fifty in a blue paisley dress and the ugliest flowered hat Randy had seen in a very long time.

In front of the lady in the ugly hat was a man in his early twenties, dressed in jeans and a gray hoodie. Both hands were in his pockets.

As the man waited his turn, the newly minted Ranger behind him sized him up.

The man was nervous. Although Randy couldn't see his face, he could see the man's head moving slightly from side to side. Randy imagined his eyeballs flitting back and forth rapidly as he constantly checked out his surroundings.

The man couldn't stand still. He rocked back and forth, shifting his weight from his left foot to his right and back again.

Two minutes ticked slowly by.

The nervous man continued to rock. The lady's hat continued to be ugly. Randy continued to wait for the right moment to make his move.

Tony Wagner, Randy's partner, took up a position just inside the bank's door and surveyed everyone else in the lobby. His hand rested on the firearm beneath his jacket as he tried to assess whether the nervous man might have an accomplice in the bank.

Finally, the second teller on the right motioned for the man to approach her window.

As he walked toward her, his right hand came out of his pocket. It held what appeared to be a note.

His left hand remained in his pocket, but Randy could clearly see the butt of a handgun. It appeared to be a chrome revolver, probably a .38.

Randy could easily see the sense of alarm on the Teller's face as she read the note. A middle-aged woman with fair skin, she flushed bright red when she realized she was being robbed.

The man pulled out his weapon just far enough to show the teller he was for real.

"Do what the note says and you won't get hurt," he whispered.

At that moment, the robber felt the hard grip of Randy's left hand on the back of his arm, just above the elbow, forcing his arm downward into his jacket's pocket.

He could not pull the gun from his pocket with his arm being forced downward. He couldn't wiggle free because Randy had the full force of his tall and muscular frame pressing the bandit into the counter in front of him. He started to yell out and start cursing whoever had him pinned, but then felt cold hard steel on his neck, just below and behind his ear.

That got his attention rather quickly.

Randy said in a very calm, almost soothing voice, "That cold metal you feel is the receiving end of my service weapon. You have a choice to make, my friend. If you continue to struggle, a nine millimeter slug is going to make a big mess of the inside of your head. Or, you can relax and cooperate and save your own life today.

"It doesn't matter to me. Either way, I'm going home tonight. The only question is whether you're going to the jail or to the morgue."

Randy felt the man relax, then start to whimper.

"I'm sorry. I just needed a fix, that's all. All my family and friends have deserted me. Nobody will help me anymore. I'm desperate."

"The help they were giving you was no help at all, my friend. Every time they gave you money for that junk they walked you a few steps closer to your grave. The kind of help you need is in jail, where they can make you get clean, then teach you some things to help you stay that way."

Chapter 3

The would-be robber wasn't the only one sobbing. The teller almost passed out when she saw Randy come up behind the thief and pull out his gun.

The lady in the ugly hat gasped when she saw the gun and waddled toward the door. She decided she'd do her banking business another day.

Randy could see the state the teller was in and tried to calm her nerves.

"Texas Ranger, ma'am. I'd show you my badge but I'm kind of busy at the moment. Have you pressed the alarm yet?"

"Yes, sir."

"Very good. Please get yourself and the rest of the tellers down and in a safe place. He still has his finger on the trigger of his gun. If he twitches, he might just get off a shot before I have to knock him cold. Chances are it'll go right into his foot, but it might miss and ricochet somewhere else. I'd prefer it if nobody got accidentally shot today."

Ranger Wagner called out from the door.

"I'll run interference for you, Randy, if you've got him under control."

"I've got him. Thanks, Tony."

Tony had his weapon pointed at the floor when two Austin police cars came around opposite corners and braked to a halt in front of the bank.

Three officers rushed into the bank, guns drawn, to find Tony brandishing his Texas Ranger badge in front of him.

"Texas Rangers. The man with the gun is a good guy."

One APD officer guarded the door, in case he was being had. The other two rushed over to Randy and the gunman.

"Be careful," Randy told them. "He's got his hand on a gun in his left pocket."

The two policemen took up positions on either side of the man and at slightly different angles so neither would be in the line of fire. Their weapons were aimed just beneath the man's shoulder blades.

Randy asked, "You got 'im?"

"We got 'im."

Randy backed away, leveling his weapon at the back of the man's head. He prayed he wouldn't have to pull the trigger.

The officer on the robber's left commanded, "Don't do anything stupid. Take your hand, and your hand only, out of your pocket, very slowly. Do it now."

The man complied. His hand was shaking almost uncontrollably.

"Now, both hands on the counter. Do it now."

The officer stepped behind the man and kicked his feet apart with his boot. Then he placed him in cuffs and patted him down.

Randy holstered his weapon, then stuck his head over the counter.

"It's clear. You folks can come out now."

Out from under desks behind the counter, several tellers and other bank employees emerged.

The Austin PD officers introduced themselves to Randy.

Their sergeant came up and patted Randy on the back.

"Good work, Ranger. We've been trying to catch this guy for weeks. He's been hitting convenience stores every time he needed a fix. At the last one, the clerk pulled a gun on him. I guess he decided to up his game and thought banks might be a safer bet."

"Glad to help."

The hapless crook was led to the street and placed in the back of a patrol car.

The officers busied themselves inside the bank, taking witness statements, while the sergeant stood on the sidewalk watching the prisoner and smoking a cigarette.

Randy asked Tony to wait for him.

"Hey Sergeant, do you mind if I talk to him for just a minute?"

"Don't know why you would, but it doesn't matter to me."

Randy opened the front passenger door and sat on the seat, his feet resting on the curb outside.

In the same calm and soothing voice he'd used before Randy asked, "What's your name, partner?"

"Jason. Jason Martinez."

"Jason, what are you using that makes you hurt so bad you'd risk your life to get it?"

"Ice. Crystal meth."

"How much are you using?"

"Three grams a day when I can get it."

Randy let out a low whistle.

"You got a record, Jason?"

"Yes, sir. Eighteen months for aggravated robbery, then six months for assault."

"You know you're going away for several years this time, right?"

"Maybe that's what I need. Maybe this will finally be my chance to get clean. I can't do it on my own. I've tried. It's just too damn hard."

"I'll tell you what, Jason. I'm going to give my card to this sergeant here. I'll ask him to make sure it goes into your record at booking and that your attorney gets it. You tell your attorney to tell me the disposition of your case. And to let me know if you need anything while you're locked up. I won't make you any promises, but I'll see if I can make things a little easier on you and your family while you're away."

"Okay. But why?"

"Because I read people very well, Jason. I can sense that you're a good kid who just got caught up in something bad.

"I think you can be that good kid again.

"And I believe in second chances."

Randy wished the man well and closed the car door. He took a business card from his pocket and handed it to the sergeant.

"You're making a mistake," the sergeant said. "Kids like that, all they know how to do is take from people. First strangers. Then their families, and then their friends. After all their friends and families disappear, they go back to stealing from strangers until they get caught. I've seen it more times than I can count."

"Maybe there's a better way," Randy said. "Maybe if we stay in touch with them after they get out we can help keep them out."

"Have you passed out your card to many arrestees?"

"No. Actually, this is the first time."

"Good luck with your theory, Ranger. I hope it works out for you."

As Randy walked away, the sergeant opened the car door again.

"Consider yourself lucky, man. I think you just met the first Ranger with a heart."

Chapter 4

The life of a Texas Ranger is a noble one. But it's not a life which makes one rich.

Randy grew up in a home that was modest by anyone's standard, the smallest house on the block in the center of a neighborhood struggling to achieve middle class status.

His early years were unremarkable, in that Randy was average in almost every way. His C average grades certainly did nothing to impress his elementary school teachers, and the school's athletic coaches weren't beating a path to his door to sign him up.

But then again, Randy wasn't trying to impress anyone. His philosophy in those years was to have good clean fun and to let the overachievers overachieve.

For Randy wasn't planning to be a rocket scientist, or a Wall Street banker, or a doctor or a lawyer.

Randy knew, from the time he could walk, that he would be just like his father.

When he was a tiny tot of two years Randy's father Jacob went through the house, tossing sofa cushions here and there and upturning furniture.

"Jake," his wife exclaimed, "What on earth are you looking for?"

"My badge. I can't find my badge. I can't go in without it."

The badge was gold in color, with the word TEXAS engraved across the top of a circular band.

RANGER was emblazoned across the bottom, and in the center of the band was a Texas five-point star.

The badge was nothing special to look at. Its luster had worn off long before, and it was nicked and pitted. If one were to look closely they'd have noticed that it was slightly bent, and that the pin had been soldered slightly off-center on the back.

It was not perfect by any means, and to anyone not named Maloney it was nothing special.

But in Jacob's house it was very special indeed.

It was the badge passed down from Wilford P. Maloney. He was the first of five Rangers in the Maloney family. And the first to wear this particular badge.

It was worn and pitted and lacking of luster, sure. But so is pretty much everything that's more than a hundred years old. That's outlived four of its wearers. That's struck fear into the hearts of many bad men and brought relief to many of those oppressed.

On this day, Jacob was fit to be tied.

He had other badges he could have worn to work. Shiny badges that were cranked out by machine instead of by hand. Badges that had no pits or scars or imperfections.

Or character.

Sure, he could have worn another badge to work on this day and continued his search later.

But the badge, to Jacob, was much more than a piece of metal.

It was a family tradition. A display of a proud heritage. A good luck charm of sorts.

It was a reminder that all four of the Maloney men who'd worn the badge had lived through hell and had survived. Wilford P. was stabbed by a Comanche warrior and lived. He later had his horse shot out from under him on the prairie outside of Lubbock. The horse fell atop his leg and broke it in two places. Yet the wily Ranger somehow managed to send the shooter to meet his maker, then got himself two miles to the nearest doctor to have his leg set.

Wilford P.'s son and Randy's great grandfather Silas was shot on the back. An ambush down San Antonio way. He spent two months in the hospital, the badge pinned on his bed pillow. He always said it was the badge's mojo which kept him from dying.

Silas was the very last Texas Ranger forced to retire at ten years, before the Rangers did away with the policy.

Silas had but one child, Bill, who became a Ranger five years after Silas put the badge in a drawer for safekeeping.

Bill vowed to be the first Ranger Maloney in three generations to finish out his career without being shot or stabbed or abused in any other way by outlaws or evildoers.

He was shot on three different occasions, a total of seven wounds, during his twenty-one year career.

Bill tried to dissuade Jacob from signing up.

"I was lucky," he told his son. "I put your mother through hell each and every night. She cringed every time the phone rang. I probably shorted her life. It was wrong of me to do that, son. I had no right to. You can learn from my mistake. You can put this whole legacy thing to rest. You can get a normal job. A truck driver. A store clerk. Something where you can go to work each day with a reasonable expectation of coming home again. Something that doesn't make your wife worry about the day she becomes a widow and her kids become fatherless. You can stop the madness, Jake."

Jake didn't stop the madness. He signed up to be a Ranger on his eighteenth birthday.

When his father pinned the badge on his chest he whispered in his son's ear.

"I'm proud of you, boy. But damn it, I wish you'd have listened to me. I will pray to God every day that He keep you safe."

God was apparently listening that day. Jacob had never suffered as much as a scratch at the hands of a bad man. He didn't attribute it to God's blessing, though. For Jacob was a superstitious sort by nature. He believed that the badge was a powerful talisman, capable of magical powers of protection. He thought it was the badge, and not God or circumstance, which had kept each successive Ranger in the family from being killed.

And now that badge was missing.

He fumed and tore his house apart searching, before Randy's mother Minnie thought to ask her son.

"Randy, have you seen your daddy's badge?"

Randy sheepishly waddled, pigeon-toed and unsteady, to his bedroom and retrieved the badge from his bed where he'd been playing with it.

He ran back into the living room and handed it over to his father.

"I like," he proudly announced. "It shiny."

Even then, before he knew what a Ranger was or did, Randy wanted the badge for his very own.

Chapter 5

Randy attended Texas Tech University. By then he'd grown into a strapping young man, and people told him constantly he was a spitting image of James Arness.

The first time he'd heard the observation he'd asked, "Who?"

"The guy who played Marshal Dillon on *Gunsmoke*."

"*Gunsmoke?* Is that a movie?"

Randy didn't watch a lot of television as a child. He was always outside with his friends playing cops and robbers.

Besides growing into a handsome young man, he also matured a bit emotionally. So did his study habits and he received a bachelor's degree in criminal justice after just three years.

On his twenty-first birthday.

Most of his fellow graduates went on benders. But not Randy. Randy was a teetotaler. Not because he considered himself better or more responsible than others. He'd tried alcohol. And cigarettes too. He just didn't like either one of them.

So on his twenty-first birthday, when he went out with his friends to celebrate both his becoming a man and graduating from college, Randy was the designated driver.

By four a.m. he got the last of his drunken buddies to their houses and tucked safely inside.

Then he went home and started packing.

Two days later he was in Austin, his head shaved clean and undergoing a grueling five mile run.

It was Day 1 of Ranger Academy.

He was three months away from getting his badge.

He would carry on a family tradition.

Another tradition, though, would go unfulfilled. Jacob would not be there when Randy graduated to hang that tarnished and well worn badge on his son.

Jacob died the previous year of colon cancer.

Minnie, an introvert in every sense of the word, hated being the center of attention. She hated being on any stage at any time and for any reason. The mere thought of a large group of people watching her made her shiver.

But she would take Jacob's place. She would pin that badge on her son's chest. It was what Jacob would have wanted.

Secretly, Minnie hoped that Randy would wash out of the Ranger Academy. The family's luck had lasted too long, she believed. Had been stretched too thin. Every winning streak eventually comes to an end. She knew in her heart as long as the Maloneys kept wearing that damn badge, that luck was going to run out on one of them. One of them was going on watch one day and wasn't coming back home.

She didn't consider herself a selfish woman by any means. But she didn't want to be the mother who accepted that American flag and had to listen to her son's eulogy. About how he was a gallant hero in the eyes of Texas.

She didn't want to watch her future daughter-in-law accept the flag for her grandson's sacrifice either.

She was hoping that Randy would wash out of the Academy. So he could do something safe. Like be an accountant. A stockbroker. Hell, she'd even let him be a fireman and rescue people from burning buildings.

As long as her only child didn't wear that damn badge. Didn't go to work each and every day knowing that he'd be around people who hated him enough to kill him. Or who hated the badge and what it represented.

Minnie needn't have worried about Randy. She should have worried about herself.

Two years to the day after she pinned that damned star on Randy's chest he called her to invite her to dinner.

"I want to take out the sweetest, most beautifulest mom in the whole State of Texas. And probably the universe as well."

"Um, Randy… I don't think there's such a word as beautifulest."

"There has to be. No other word describes you adequately. I'll call the dictionary people tomorrow and have them add it, with your photo just above it."

That was Randy. He always had a kind word to say about everyone, and even when the flattery was false it still made people smile.

He wasn't smiling when he went to pick her up and found her dead on the kitchen floor.

Heart failure, the medical examiner said in the autopsy report. Due to a congenital heart defect that had gone undiagnosed for all of her forty five years.

Randy saw something else in the autopsy report as well. *Contributing factor: hypertension.*

High blood pressure. Caused, no doubt, from being a Ranger's wife. Maybe not entirely. For many years Minnie had been extremely introverted, almost afraid to speak with strangers. She kept inside herself, kept her problems and troubles bottled up as well.

Holding one's feelings within themselves so firmly did terrible things to the human body.

So did biting one's tongue when she wanted to scream at her husband to find a new line of work.

A line of work that wouldn't cause her to cry herself to sleep each night, wondering if that was the night her husband wouldn't come home.

If that was the night a police chaplain would rap on the door at three a.m., causing her to sit bolt upright in bed, knowing.

Randy couldn't do anything to bring his mother back, or to take back the hell that her life must have been.

The next best thing, the only thing he could do in tribute to his beloved mother, was to end the legacy.

The Rangers still offered a ten year retirement plan. The early out, they called it. It was a plan which offered few benefits other than an increased life expectancy. But that was okay. He could do something else.

Randy decided to end his career after ten years. He'd have plenty of time to do what he'd always dreamed of doing. Plenty of time to help right the wrongs in his beloved State of Texas.

He'd retire at thirty one. Still young enough to date. Still young enough to fall in love. Still young enough to have a family.

But his son, if he had one, would never see him go off to work with a badge on his chest and a gun on his hip.

His son, if he had one, would never hear his mother crying late at night and begging God to just let Randy be late. Not to let him be lying dead in a street somewhere.

His son would not grow up the son of a lawman. He'd grow up the son of an accountant. Or a banker. Or a real estate agent.

He'd never be the hero to his son that Jacob was to Randy.

But hopefully his son would have his mother for more than twenty three short years.

With no family left and no girlfriend to hold him back, Randy poured himself into his career. He wanted to be the best Ranger that Texas ever had. He wanted to work his last shift after ten years and visit the grave of his great great grandfather, old Wilford P. Maloney himself.

He planned to thank old W.P. for the fine example he'd set for the Maloney family. For leading the way and for starting a legacy that five generations fulfilled.

But he'd say it was time for the legacy to come to a close. That the Maloney women had suffered too much over the years and it was time to put an end to it.

He'd bury that shield in the ground over W.P.'s grave. He'd return it to its original owner.

"Thank you for the opportunity to serve my Texas," he'd tell the old man.

"But now it's somebody else's turn."

Chapter 6

Randy quickly became a rising star in the agency. His quiet demeanor won him a lot of cases. His calm and calculated way of doing his job helped gain the trust of the people he came in contact with. Whether they were frightened victims of violent crime or confidential informants on the dredges of society, they seemed to trust Randy and to take him at his word.

And that trust was well founded, for Randy was a man of impeccable integrity.

The foiled bank robbery put Randy into the media's spotlight as well. He'd been interviewed by a doll of a reporter for one of Austin's local television stations the day after the event.

He didn't want to do it, but the publicity officer told him he had to.

"Law enforcement usually gets a bad rap in the news media," he'd said. "The public complains that we don't do enough to serve them and the bad guys claim we go out of our way to be rough on them. We can't win. Well, every once in a while we get the chance to show the public the good things we do with something heroic and noncontroversial. You *will* report to KAUS-TV and you *will* do the interview and you *will* enjoy it. That's an order, Ranger."

Randy wasn't one to watch the evening news. He was usually at the gym working out or reading. So he'd never seen Melissa Rey before he walked into Studio 2.

He was instantly infatuated with her.

"What was going through your mind when you realized the man at the bank was going to rob it?"

"Well, I realized I had to stop it."

"And had you formulated a plan to do that?"

"No, I just did what felt right."

"Were you in fear of your life at any time during the event?"

"No, not really."

"How do you feel about the bank employees calling you a hero?"

"Well shucks, ma'am. I'm not a hero. The people who put on a military uniform and go off to faraway lands, they're heroes. Firemen who go into burning buildings to save others, they're heroes. Doctors and nurses who save lives each and every day and consider it routine, they're heroes. I'm just a man trying to do his job the best way he can. And, well shucks, that don't make me a hero."

If the reporter was looking for an egomaniac willing to brag on himself she was shortchanged. The truth was, Randy was a terrible candidate for an interview. But he was genuine, and likeable.

And the audience loved him.

For the next sixty days, the publicity officer had him going from here to there around the Austin area. Accepting an award for bravery from the mayor. And another one from the First Union Bank. An elementary school declared "Ranger Randy Day" and invited him to have lunch with the children and give a speech. He didn't like the speech part much, but enjoyed the time he spent with the children.

The television interview won him a couple of other things too.

It effectively got rid of the Randall moniker. Randall was replaced with a brand spanking new nickname. For many years to come, he'd be called "Ah Shucks" by his fellow Rangers.

He didn't mind it much. It was better than Randall.

He also won the heart of Melissa, who was enamored by his boyish charm, good looks and sweet nature.

The two dated, but not too seriously. He was honest from the beginning, telling her he had no plans to marry while he wore the Ranger badge.

"So give it up," she'd told him. "A man like you, you can do anything you want to do. You don't have to work in a job where your wife has to worry about you every time you go off to work."

"I can't give it up. It's in my blood. It's all I've ever wanted to do."

She tried to change his mind, but to no avail. Finally she told him her biological clock was ticking.

"I want to have children before I get too old to enjoy them. I want to have your children, but you won't marry me. I have to say goodbye."

Her leaving hurt Randy, but he knew going in that it was inevitable. He could have chosen her over his career, sure. And she was probably right. He didn't have to be a Ranger. He could have been anything.

But he'd made his choice, long before he met her.

He wished her well, promised they'd always be friends, and rode off into the proverbial sunset.

Chapter 7

Randy was transferred to a Ranger company in his hometown of Lubbock, at the base of the Texas panhandle.

Lubbock was most famous for its favorite son, rock 'n' roll singer Buddy Holly. And dust storms.

Dust storms. That's what they called them when Randy was a kid. Sometime around the time he started his senior year at Lubbock High School the local TV station provided videotape of something they called a "haboob."

"What in heck is a haboob?" Randy asked his science teacher.

"Heck if I know, Randy. Some bigwig meteorologist at the National Weather Service says it's a haboob, so I guess that's what everybody'll start calling them now. I personally don't see what was wrong with 'dust storm.'"

"Well, it'll always be a dust storm to me."

Randy was a simple guy, even back then. Ranger school hadn't changed him much. He did his job well, kept his nose clean and kept a low profile.

Many of his friends from Lubbock High hadn't even been aware there was a Texas Ranger detachment in Lubbock. Ranger Company C had been there for many years, in a small office in the Mahon Federal Building across the street from the courthouse. The office was tiny in comparison to the offices of other federal agencies who were a bit more pretentious. It was also rumored to be haunted, as Randy found out the day he reported.

"Am I working day shift or nights?" he inquired of his new commander, Major John Shultz.

"Oh, we'll work you strictly on days, unless you're on special assignment or doing a stakeout. We try to stay out of this office as much as possible during nighttime, ever since Waylor left us high and dry."

"Waylor? Who's Waylor?"

"Bob Waylor. He was a young pup, just like yourself. Kinda skittish and nervous, like a stray puppy. Used to man the office on night shift, until he finally got so much of Henry's ghost he couldn't take it anymore. Put in for a transfer to Clay County, just to get out of here."

Randy looked the major in the eye. He didn't see a hint of humor, or anything else to indicate the ghost tale was fantasy.

"Henry's ghost?"

"Henry Jenkins. He was a cowboy, died about the age of thirty two. Back in the early 1900s this part of Texas was still mostly untamed. There was a big hotel here on this spot, the Nicolett. Three stories, and the finest hotel within three hundred miles in any direction, it was said.

"Anyway, in the early teens young Henry Jenkins was a guest of the hotel and died in his bed, of pneumonia. We did some checking after Waylor skedaddled, and figured out that old Henry's bed was on the third floor, west corner, of the Nicolett Hotel.

"Right about where you're sitting right now."

Randy was unmoved. He didn't necessarily believe in ghosts. But he didn't necessarily disbelieve in them either.

The major went on.

"Anyway, there's no denying that strange things happen in this office sometimes. You'll see it yourself. Strange thumping sounds within the walls. Cold drafts, even though the windows are all sealed. Things being moved around from where you left them, even when the office is locked.

"Waylor was on night duty. He claimed all that stuff was ten times worse when the sun went down. Said he heard more, too. A man coughing and sometimes crying, even though all the other offices on the floor were locked up tighter than a drum. He said he'd hear those things several times a night, and it would make the hair on the back of his neck stand straight up. Finally he heard a man cry out, 'God help me, I'm dying.'

"He put in his papers the very next day, said he'd go to any company in the state that wasn't in Lubbock, Texas. So they sent him to Clay County. We haven't had a night shift since.

"Anyway, after he was gone, curiosity got the best of me so I did some checking. That's when I discovered that his hotel room was the same place as our office is now. Henry Jenkins, he was taken from the Nicolett Hotel when he died and was buried in a plot of land southeast of here. Turns out some ranchers donated some acreage to the newly founded city of Lubbock to use as a cemetery. Young Jenkins was the very first man buried in it.

"He didn't even have a headstone until sometime later, when the city gave him one. It said 'Here Lies Henry Jenkins, A Cowboy, About Age 32.' Seems no one knew him well enough to know exactly how old he was so they guessed."

Randy's curiosity was piqued, but just a tiny bit.

"Do you really believe all of that, sir?"

"Oh, I know it for a fact. I did the research."

"No. I mean about Henry's ghost haunting this office."

"Well, I don't know, son. I do know that there's some strange goings on here in the daytime. I can personally attest to that. As for the night time, I can't say. I never spent a night here myself.

"I'm married and old, you see. My traveling days as a Ranger are past me now. When I got this billet, I promised my wife I'd spend nights with her again to make up for all those years I couldn't. I'm a man of my word and even if I wasn't, it wouldn't matter much.

"My wife is the kind of woman you don't break a promise to. Once someone makes Nellie a promise, she holds them to it. She'd have my ass in a wringer if I ever tried to spend a night up here after telling her I wouldn't. I can tell you one thing about Henry's ghost. Ranger Waylor believed in it enough to light out of here like his horse was on fire. He even no-showed the farewell dinner we planned for him so he could get out quicker. He called us from the road to tell us to eat his plate for him, he was already halfway to his new assignment.

"I'll tell you what, though. If you want to find out for yourself, you just feel free. Your key will fit the office door any time of day and you can spend as many nights up here as you want. Just let me know how that works out for you."

Randy was always up for either a dare or a good challenge. This sounded like both.

"Let me get settled in first and I'll take you up on it."

Chapter 8

A week after his return to Lubbock, Randy went to the city's Lowrey Field to watch his Lubbock High School Westerners play the nearby town of Dimmit.

He ran into several old friends, who were skeptical about Randy's claims about being based in Lubbock.

"Hell, there ain't no Texas Rangers in Lubbock. If there were then surely we would've heard about them. Hey, Red," one of them called to another friend who happened by. "You heard tell of any Texas Rangers based here in Lubbock?"

"Hell, the Texas Rangers is a damn baseball team. Are you stupid, or what?"

Randy was flustered.

"Do you guys really have to use that kind of language? I mean, the point you're making doesn't gain any strength by adding those words. Why make women and children blush by your choice of language?"

"Oh hell, Randy. There ain't no women or children around here that don't hear those words at least ten times a day. The only one around here who don't like 'em is you. And I've never understood why. Why in hell is that, Randy?"

"I don't know, Red. I just don't think the words are necessary, that's all."

"Randy, I like you. You're a good man. I try not to use the words around you because I know you're a classy guy and because you're one of my best friends. But I think you're pulling my leg about being stationed here. There ain't no Ranger company in Lubbock, and that's for darn sure.

"Did you catch that, old friend? I said darn instead of damn. Just for you."

"Thank you, Red. I appreciate it."

Truth was, Ranger Company C kept such a low profile that many Lubbock residents would have guessed they'd have to drive all the way down to Austin, three hundred and fifty miles away, just to see a real live Ranger.

The Rangers were tasked with a variety of things, from investigating corruption among police departments and sheriff's offices to assisting federal marshals in making arrests to providing security details for visiting dignitaries and politicians.

But they were seldom written up in the local newspaper. Almost never appeared on the local nightly news.

And that was the way they preferred it. The Rangers were like the ninjas of law enforcers. When they did their job well, they were never seen, never talked about, never credited.

Randy didn't have to go to Lubbock. He was offered the opportunity to be a member of Governor John Samson's security team, but he turned it down. Other Rangers told him he was a fool. A billet with the governor, they said, was a ticket to high places in the Ranger organization later in his career.

But Randy was a simple man with a simple plan. He was to be the best Ranger Texas ever had. Then he was going to hang up his spurs and put an end to the family legacy.

Besides, Lubbock was his home. There was no other place on earth like it. Only the natives understood how special the place was. A lot of them wanted to keep it a secret. The thinking was, if the world found out what a jewel Lubbock was, outsiders would flock there. It would lose its small town feel. And that would ruin everything.

Randy left the game when his Westerners had a comfortable three touchdown lead and went to a local bar with Red and the boys. They sat at a large table in the center of the room and focused their attention on a wall-mounted television showing a college game.

He ordered a Dr. Pepper and a bag of peanuts.

"Sorry, sir. We don't have any shelled peanuts. We have some over there on the bar but they're still in the shell. I'll bring you a bowl if you don't mind shelling them."

"Ah, shucks. I don't mind shellin' 'em, if you don't mind bringin' 'em."

"'Oh, shucks?' Are you from around here?"

"Born and raised. Went to Lubbock High. Why?"

"Oh, just wonderin', that's all. We don't get a lot of guys in here saying 'oh, shucks and drinkin' Dr. Pepper."

She smiled.

"I'll go get your peanuts, Dudley Doo-Right. Be right back."

Red chuckled about "Dudley Doo-Right" and focused on a girl sitting alone at the end of the bar.

"She sure is pretty."

"Far too pretty for the likes of you, Red."

Budweiser spewed from Red's nose and he coughed heartily. After he finally caught his breath he said to his friends, "Did y'all hear that? Randy dogged me. In all the years I've known him... hell, since grade school, he's never dogged me out, not even once."

One of their buddies raised a bottle to Randy.

"Nice going, Randy. It's about time somebody shut Red up and made him choke on his beer. About damn time."

Red said, "Yeah, yeah... but Randy? Seriously? Who'd have ever thought?"

The server placed a bowl full of unshelled peanuts on the table in front of Randy and said, "These are on the house. So's the Dr. Pepper. Let me know when you need a refill of either."

"Yes ma'am. Thank you."

She walked away with the sweetest smile.

Chapter 9

Randy caught a hot case on his third day on the job. He and his partner, Tom Cohen, were called upon to investigate a small town police department in Hale County, just north of Lubbock.

There were allegations that the chief of police of a six man department was looking the other way as a Mexican drug cartel took over his town. The story went that the cartel then used the tiny town as a base to manufacture and deliver drugs not only to Lubbock, but north to Amarillo as well.

If confirmed, the charges were not only serious. They were troubling as well. For they would call to light a new tactic for Mexican drug lords. They'd always infiltrated the big and moderate sized cities. Had plied their trade with numerous well-trained officers watching out for them and breathing down their necks.

In smaller towns, with fewer and less well-trained officers, they were far more likely to practice their trade and dispense their drugs with impunity. It would also give them a safe haven to retreat to when the heat in the larger cities grew too hot to handle.

The pair of Rangers crawled into their Ford F-150 pickup and made the seventy mile drive north to the sleepy little town of Belton, population 985.

Instead of barging into the police department, tossing around accusations and demanding answers, they drove into town and pulled up to a local diner.

Their pickup truck and cowboy hats enabled them to blend in with the locals. And although neither of them knew a boll weevil from a cricket, they were able to mingle easily with the local farmers.

At least to outsiders.

They had a hearty breakfast. Bacon and eggs for Randy, Flapjacks and sausage for Tom, and made small talk with the waitress. A painfully thin woman with graying hair, Janice claimed to know everything about everybody.

"Hell, I've lived in Belton since *before* Christ was a corporal. I was the first baby born in the Belton Clinic when they opened their doors fifty seven years ago. I was the last patient they served before they closed their doors six months ago. Got taken over by some big medical corporation. Said it wasn't cost effective to keep it open any more. Said Obamacare was forcing them to consolidate their operations in the big cites, close the ones in the little towns. Now if that don't beat all.

"Now we gotta go down to Lubbock or up to Amarillo, even to get a damn prescription filled. It just ain't right."

Then she caught herself.

"Oh, I'm sorry. I tend to get sidetracked. The short answer to your question... yes, I know pretty much everything that goes on around here. What kind of information were you guys looking for, exactly?"

"We're bounty hunters. We'd appreciate it if you'd keep what we tell you to yourself."

There weren't a lot of other customers in the diner on Highway 87. It had been rather slow all morning, and Janice loved to be the first in on the latest gossip.

She looked around, then sat down next to Randy and across the booth from Tom.

In a conspiratorial tone she said, "Go on. Who ya lookin' for?"

"Can't give you any names. Just descriptions. Names wouldn't do you any good, since they've each got a dozen aliases. Mexicans. Not locals. The ones who come up here from Mexico and keep to themselves. They don't speak any English, or very little of it. They probably just show their faces in town occasionally to buy a meal or to buy beer or smokes at a local convenience store. Have you seen anyone like that?"

"Hell, mister. This here's cotton country. We see so many of those kind you can't even count 'em all. Especially when it comes time to do the strippin'. They're all over the place."

"I don't mean laborers. I mean men that drive nice trucks. Wear decent clothes. Not suits, but not ragged discount store jeans either. And watches. Men with money wear nice watches, even when they're trying to look like everybody else."

"Say, what'd these guys do, anyway?"

"They were in jail in El Paso for bank robbery. They bonded out and vamoosed. The bond agent wants 'em back so he's not on the hook for their bonds."

"Maybe they vamoosed back to Mexico, where they came from."

"Nope. We have them on video at a convenience store in San Angelo. They bought cigarettes and got friendly with a night clerk who spoke fluent Spanish. Said they were headed this way. That they knew some people hereabouts and they were gonna hide out here for awhile and lay low."

Janice suddenly remembered her rent was due in a few days. And her tips had been pretty abysmal of late.

"Say, this bond agent of yours. Is he offering any kind of reward for these guys?"

Tom, who'd been spinning the tail, turned to Randy and asked him, "What do you think? Do you think old Saul would cut loose some money for our friend here if her information led us to our guys?"

Randy shrugged.

"Well, I don't know. We'd have to ask him. But I'm pretty sure he'll be tickled pink to get his guys back. And you know Saul. He can be a very generous man when he's happy."

Tom smiled and agreed.

"Yes, sirree. A very generous man indeed."

"I'll tell you what," Janice said. "I've seen several guys, like the ones you describe. They dress like everybody else but they drive new Silverados and Ram trucks. Diamond studs in their ears and Rolex watches. Not the fake ones either. Their English is lousy. They usually have to point at the pictures on the menu to tell me what they want. And they usually pay with fifty dollar bills and run us out of change.

"They don't come in here but a couple of times a week or so. But how about if the next time I see 'em I sneak outside for a smoke and write down their license plate numbers for you. And see what direction they go when they driv e off. Would that help?"

"Sure it would, ma'am. We'll check back in a couple of days."

Chapter 10

It was actually four days before the Rangers made it back to Belton. They were asked to provide backup to a team serving warrants down Abilene way. And a Ranger never refuses a call for help from one of their own.

Janice was antsy when they walked in and sat at the same table.

She took their drink order, but gave no indication she'd ever seen either of them before. Didn't even make eye contact.

Not with the Rangers, anyway. But her eyes kept flitting to a booth in the corner where four hombres were seated, laughing and conversing loudly in rapid Spanish.

Their boots were a dead giveaway. Ranger Tom had told her about the fancy watches and shiny new pickups. But it never occurred to him to mention the boots.

Most of Janice's Hispanic customers were farm hands or ranch hands. It was easy to tell the difference. The farm hands wore tennis shoes or sneakers. Not Nikes or Reeboks. But department store brands. Cheap ones, for lack of a better term.

They were more suited for working in the fields all day long, stripping cotton from thorny plants in muddy fields in hundred degree heat.

But soft shoes weren't suited for working a ranch. And any rancher worth his salt wouldn't allow them.

A ranch environment was much different than a farming operation, both in the types of duties involved and hazards faced.

A soft sneaker wouldn't protect a worker's foot if it got stomped on by a steer. But a sturdy leather boot might. A man hopping off a hay wagon after feeding a herd might turn his ankle in a running shoe. He was less likely to in a boot.

And there was a certain tradition among ranchers that was equally as important as efficiency and safety. A ranch hand should look and act like a ranch hand. Not like a damn city-slicker or a ragamuffin.

There wasn't a ranch owner in the county who'd cotton to a hand wearing sweat pants and sneakers. All the hands knew this, so blue jeans and boots were the norm.

So it was easy to tell, while walking around town, which of the brown-skinned laborers worked in farming and which worked on ranches. The county had roughly an equal share of both.

It wasn't so easy to tell which of the workers were legal and which ones weren't. And it didn't really matter. The crops had to be brought in, the steers had to be wrangled. Farmers and ranchers in this area didn't cotton to the federal, or even the state government telling them who they could and couldn't hire. They didn't much care if a man had a green card or not. They only cared whether he did his job. They paid in cash and asked no questions. It had been that way in Texas for generations, and would likely stay that way.

While it was easy to tell which brown-skinned men in Belton were ranch hands, it was easier to tell that the men at the booth in Janice's diner weren't.

Tom had forgotten to mention the boots. The difference was easy to spot.

A ranch hand's boots were cheap. A no-frills brand. And they were creased and dirty and worn. And just as likely their seams were embedded with cow shit.

The boots at the booth were altogether different.

They were made of alligator and rattlesnake. The pointed toes were much more pronounced, almost sharp enough to cut someone's throat. They were spit-shined, and had never been within half a mile of cow shit at any time, nor were they likely to ever be.

Most telling, though, was the style.

These boots were lined with silver trim, not unlike the chrome on an old Chevy.

It was a style of boots made in Mexico, for Mexicans. They were hard to find in ranching country, because they were too fancy for ranch work. They were simply too flimsy to stand up to the task.

Randy and Tom knew why Janice was nervous.

The men they'd asked about... the men Janice promised to watch out for... were having a good time just thirty feet away from them.

Randy gave no hint he knew, just as she'd given no hint they were there.

"Hello, miss. I'd just like a Dr. Pepper to go. In a bottle, please. And a bag of salted peanuts."

She looked over to Tom.

"I'll have a coke, also in a bottle. And no nuts for me. That's just too weird for this cowboy."

Chapter 11

Randy opened the small packet of peanuts and dumped them into his bottle of Dr. Pepper. They caused it to fizz slightly, but it wasn't in danger of overflowing the bottle.

Tom watched as Randy took a swig and said, "Tell me again why you do that?"

"It was just something I watched my dad do when I was a small boy. A lot of his friends did it too. I tried it and liked it, and before I knew it all my friends were doing it too."

Tom huffed.

"Just curious, but did all of your friends accompany you on the same space ship from Planet Weirdo?"

"Hey, don't knock it 'til you try it."

"Yeah, whatever. Like that's gonna ever happen."

"It will. Your curiosity will get the best of you. You'll see. But when you do, be sure the peanuts are salted. Spanish peanuts are the best. Those are the little round red ones. And be sure you eat them after your Dr. Pepper is finished. They'll be a bit softer from being moistened, and they're amazing."

"If you say so."

"I say so. You'll get hooked on it. You'll start adding them whenever you have a Dr. Pepper. And wherever you go, people will see you do it, and they'll know two things."

"Okay, I'll bite. What two things?"

"First of all, they'll know you're a man of above average intelligence. Because those are the only type of men who take the peanut challenge."

"I see. And the second thing?"

"They'll know you've been to West Texas."

They got up to leave and left a ten dollar bill on the table to pay their tab.

As they walked out the door, Randy took his cell phone out of his pocket and pretended to answer a call.

But there was no one on the other line. As they walked through the parking lot toward their pickup, he scanned the lot and the other vehicles contained in it. He saw one in particular that was his target, and walked slowly past it.

As he passed it he finished his pretend call and lowered the phone from his ear. Just before he placed it into his pocket, though, he used the phone to snap a photograph of the truck's license plate.

"How'd you know that Silverado was their truck," Tom asked as they were climbing into their own pickup truck.

"Because it's clean and it's tricked out. And because it's a Chevy."

Randy was a Ford guy himself. Always had been. But even back in high school, when he hung out with his Hispanic friends in the Arnett Benson section of Lubbock, he couldn't help but notice an irrefutable fact.

They all preferred Chevrolets.

He didn't know why. Maybe it was a tradition passed down from father to son. Maybe they preferred the sleek styling of the Monte Carlos and the Camaros.

Randy didn't know. He asked a couple of his friends one day.

"Hey, how come you guys all drive Chevrolets?"

Jesse Martinez looked at Luis Castillo, then shrugged his shoulders.

"Heck, I don't know. How come all gringos drive Fords?"

Randy didn't know.

"Heck, I don't know. I guess it just works out that way."

"Then why ask why? It's the way of the world. Pass the peanuts, my friend. I'm all out."

The pair got into their own truck and pulled out of the diner. They drove a little farther into the bowels of Belton, down a couple of residential streets and past an ancient public library. Behind the library Randy parked and Tom took a pair of Bushnell binoculars from behind the seat.

He focused on the diner, almost four blocks away now. The tricked out Chevy Silverado was no longer in view, but it didn't matter. There was only one way in and out of the parking lot, and he could see the lot's driveway.

Now it was just a matter of time.

Chapter 12

While they waited the two talked of Ranger Mike Waylor, the man who'd been frightened away from Lubbock by Henry Jenkins' ghost.

"The major told me you were going to spend the night in the office and check it out for yourself," Tom asked. "Is that true, or was he just pulling my leg?"

"I don't believe I told him I would. I believe I told him I might. It's a curious tale, and I'm a curious sort by nature. I'd kinda like to see if there's anything to the story."

"Do you believe in ghosts?"

"Well, I don't rightly know, Tom. Not really. But I don't really disbelieve in them either."

"What the hell does that mean?"

Randy winced just a bit.

"Sorry. What does that mean?"

"Well, I believe there are a lot of things out there that we just don't know much about. One theory is as good as the next one, I suppose. At least until it's proven to be false. As for what happens after death, it's kinda hard to prove one way or another."

"Do you believe in God, Randy?"

"Certainly."

"Don't you think that by believing in God, then believing in ghosts at the same time is blasphemy?"

"Not at all. The Bible says that the faithful will die and walk the golden streets of heaven for all eternity. And that sinners will go to a place of eternal damnation. But it doesn't say when. It doesn't say immediately after death. It also makes mention of purgatory, or a type of way station. Maybe those who are not righteous enough to be admitted to heaven right away spend time in purgatory while awaiting their eternal fate. Maybe the ghosts we sometimes see on earth are merely residents of purgatory who are awaiting a decision on where their souls will spend eternity."

"Hey, they're on the move."

"Yep."

Randy turned the Ford's ignition key and the engine sprang to life.

Their suspects turned right coming out of the parking lot and headed away from them. Randy pulled away from the library and proceeded in the same direction, but at a slower pace.

The Rangers had a tail policy which differed from most law enforcement agencies.

Most agencies had several units involved in a tail. They were able to break off frequently, handing control over to a different car. That car would tail the suspect for a short time, then break off and hand off to a third car. Sometimes there were up to five cars involved, all working closely by radio in a carefully orchestrated process. The end result, when done properly, was to tail the suspect without him suspecting it.

The Texas Rangers used a different strategy. It was borne of necessity, for they simply didn't have enough agents in the field to perform such a maneuver.

But they did generally work in pairs when on a case.

The Rangers' strategy was simple. One suspect vehicle, one Ranger vehicle. But the follow vehicle stayed back until the suspect vehicle was almost out of view, then used a spotter to keep him in sight.

Since Randy was at the wheel, Tom by default became the spotter. He took the binoculars and focused in on the Chevy, now over half a mile in front of them.

"Okay, I've got good visual. You can back off a little bit more."

In the rear view mirror of the suspect's truck, Randy and Tom were but a speck in the background, blending in with a myriad of other specks. Each time the suspects turned, Tom made note of a landmark at that particular intersection.

"Turn right at the yellow billboard," he might say. Or, "Turn left at the 7-Eleven."

By giving the driver his marching orders as they went, Tom could keep his eyes on the prize instead of looking around for street signs.

Another aspect of the Rangers' tail policy was for the driver to stay in contact with local authorities by radio, generally on a secure tactical channel, to keep the locals advised of their tail.

Randy and Tom chose not to do that in this case since the local police chief, Ron Bennett, was suspected to be part of the problem.

That being the case, there would be no local backup should Randy and Tom run into trouble. The local cops didn't even know they were here. They were on their own, in every sense of the word, and they knew it.

So they needed to be careful.

The suspect vehicle pulled to the shoulder of Highway 87 and put on its blinker, signaling its intent to turn onto Farm to Market Road 1348.

Farm to Market roads were seldom traveled, except by the farmers and ranchers who lived or worked down that particular road. Any vehicle at all which traveled down the road would be looked at with suspicion. A strange vehicle nobody could identify would be even more suspect.

Tom gave Randy his updated instructions.

"Fall back more. Traffic is thinning out. Slow down and turn at the third telephone pole on the right."

Then the Rangers got lucky.

As Tom watched through the binoculars, their suspects turned onto FM 1348, then took a hard left after a quarter mile onto a private road.

Tom had no idea where he was. But he knew the suspects were on a private road because their truck was kicking up a cloud of dust.

They were driving up the long caliche driveway of a rural ranch house.

"Scratch that," Tom said. "They're home. Forget the right turn. Go up a few miles and turn around. We'll go back to Lubbock and spend some time on SLEN."

As they continued on Highway 87, a quarter mile away from and adjacent to the ranch house, Tom continued to watch the pickup. He saw it come to a stop and four men exiting. They walked to the front of the house and were climbing its steps when Tom lost visual.

Seven minutes later, after they turned around and headed south toward Lubbock, he noted that the pickup was still in the yard but the men were nowhere in sight.

Their prey had gone home to roost.

Chapter 13

SLEN, or Secure Law Enforcement Network, was the Texas Ranger's go-to source for information on anything and everything.

Randy rolled his office chair over to the terminal and logged in, Tom looking over his shoulder.

Step one was to identify the ranch where their suspects were hanging out.

They had no address. But they didn't really need one. Addresses were for amateurs, and they were part of the elite law enforcement body for the finest state in the union.

Randy clicked on the icon for satellite images.

First he got an overview of the Texas panhandle, then zoomed in slightly on State Highway 87. He followed it north of Lubbock and north of Plainview, then zoomed in on a tiny speck.

The town of Belton.

There wasn't much to the town, even when one was there. The view from an orbiting satellite reflected even less. It would have been easy for Randy to overlook the tiny town as just a cluster of trees and tiny buildings in a vast sea of nothingness, were Randy not sure exactly where to look.

He zoomed in.

He saw the diner where Janice was probably fuming, wondering why they'd taken off in such a hurry.

He spotted the oak tree beside the old public library. The one they'd parked under while waiting for the Silverado to emerge from the parking lot.

He followed Highway 87 north until he found Farm to Market Road 1348, and the mysterious ranch house just off of it.

And there, as clear as could be, was the Silverado pickup, parked in roughly the same place they'd seen it pull up earlier.

Randy looked in the corner of the screen to see how old the satellite image was. It was dated July tenth. Two weeks before.

Whether they belonged at the ranch house legally, or had occupied it by force, they'd been there at least two weeks.

He knocked down the tab and clicked on another icon, this time for a Department of Motor Vehicle search. This one was a link to a national database, and he typed "Texas" into the search field to narrow his search.

A new screen popped up. The background showed an armadillo crossing a rural highway in what looked to be the big bend region of Texas. In the background was a field of Texas Bluebonnets. Randy's mother's favorite flowers and still one of the prettiest Randy had ever seen.

He typed in "CWB-966" and transmitted.

Five seconds later he was reading information about the Silverado's registered owner, a man named Ronald Smith, at 1755 Spencer Avenue in Amarillo, Texas.

He doubted that one of the Hispanic men at the diner was named Ronald Smith. And the ranch house where he and Tom had last seen the suspects definitely wasn't in Amarillo.

Tom said, "Cross-reference him in the TDCJ database."

TDJC was the Texas Department of Criminal Justice. The state prison system. If Ronald Smith, 1755 Spencer Avenue in Amarillo had ever done time in Texas, he'd be there.

Randy's fingers flew across the keys and as if by magic, a mug shot appeared on the screen.

Ronald Smith was in his late twenties and already balding.

"Probably inbred," Tom huffed.

Randy countered, "Actually, male pattern baldness is hereditary, usually on the mother's side, and usually skips at least one generation."

"Yeah, well, I like my version better."

Balding or not, Ronald Smith definitely wasn't one of the men they'd seen at the diner, or getting out at the ranch house.

Tom whistled as he scanned Smith's long rap sheet. Although not quite twenty nine, he'd already done four stints in prison. All for drug crimes.

The latest, for possession of six grams of cocaine with the intent to distribute, earned him a five year sentence.

He was paroled after two, just three months before.

"That," opined Tom, "is a big part of the drug problem. We spend all this time catching these suckers and the soft-hearted fools on the parole boards keep letting them back out again."

It was a major complaint not only among Rangers, but with virtually every other law enforcement agency in the country.

"Okay. Now what?"

"Well, we know where they're at. And I doubt they're going anywhere. Let's petition for a wiretap and see who they're talking to. We'll go out at night and plant a long range camera across the highway, where they're not likely to find it, and since there's no place to hide and do surveillance. Then let's let them stew for a few days and see if we can get the police chief on audio or video meeting with them.

"While we're waiting for that to happen, we can set up shop down the road and see if we can get some intel on where they go when they're not at the ranch."

"You got anything pressing here in Lubbock? Anything that can't wait for a couple of weeks?"

"Nope. Nothing except spend a night or two here trying to talk the ghost of old Henry Jenkins to find another place to haunt."

"I reckon old Henry will wait. Let's rent a couple of rooms at a motel on the north side. If they make us and turn the tables on us, they may tail us back to Lubbock. I'd much rather them follow us to a cheap motel and think we're a couple of rivals than tail us back to the federal building and think we might be coppers."

"Sounds good to me, my friend. Let's go fishing."

Chapter 14

Randy checked into the Slumber Inn on Highway 87 and collapsed atop the bed. He hadn't slept well for a couple of nights and it had been a trying day. His plan was to go to bed early and try to get a restful night's sleep, for he knew the case was heating up.

For the next few days he needed to be at the top of his game.

One of the things they'd taught him at the academy was that something always goes wrong in a long-term surveillance. It's the one constant in the surveillance game. No matter what your plan is, no matter how well you prepare, something will always go wrong.

A camera battery will fail at a critical time. Just before the handoff of cash takes place, an idiot in a mail truck will park it between the camera and its targets.

Or, the worst of the worst, the bad guys will figure out they're being watched and will quash whatever deal is in the works.

Or just leave and do it elsewhere.

They'd told Randy and the others at the academy that such things are unavoidable. And that the best way to deal with them is to expect them, be flexible, and to deal with them as best they could. And to always, without exception, to keep *Job 1* in mind.

Job 1, in Ranger lingo, was to always live to fight another day.

There were a lot of Texas Ranger heroes through the years. Men who'd risked their lives for the cause. Men whose circumstance, and days, had finally run out on them. Men who'd made the ultimate sacrifice in the name of Texas justice.

A lot of rangers had died in the line of duty since the Rangers' inception.

And the Rangers frowned upon that.

It wasn't that the Rangers didn't appreciate the sacrifices those men made. And they relished telling and retelling the stories of how this Ranger or that died at the tip of a Comanche spear, or by the gun of a legendary outlaw.

But they preferred their Rangers alive.

They got a lot more work done that way.

From the first day at the academy it was drilled into the heads of the Ranger candidates: nothing is worth the life of your fellow Rangers. Nothing is worth the cost of *your* life. Heroism is neither expected nor wanted.

And recklessness in the name of heroism would not be tolerated.

In the early days of the Rangers, bravado was an admirable trait. Men were different then, and so were circumstances. There was no such thing as radio backup. Men were hired with the understanding they'd be placing their lives at risk each and every day. And that one day their luck would likely run out.

That was why, in the early days of the agency, a Ranger was retired at full pension after only ten years. It was thought that a man who made it that far was incredibly lucky. And that his days were almost certainly numbered.

In modern times, bravado was frowned upon. In the twenty first century law enforcement was a completely different ball game.

These days there were smart guns. Bullet proof body armor. Bullet proof driver's side windows on patrol cars. Agencies which no longer thought it was an inconvenience to provide ready backup to their counterparts. With the understanding that their counterparts would someday be called upon to return the favor.

These days Rangers were much better at communicating with one another. And in formulating well thought out plans before beginning a new operation.

And in analyzing the situation as it progressed. And making adjustments as needed to keep their heroes safe.

Even the biggest risk: the small number of Rangers when compared with other law enforcement agencies, was addressed.

That was where the team policy came from. Any Ranger performing an investigation where even the remotest possibility of violence was present would have a partner by his side.

The thinking was that two heads were better than one. And two guns were too.

So Randy was uneasy. But he couldn't say why. The possibility of getting wounded or killed on the job were remote. He and Tom worked well together. They were together for only a short time, yet read each other very well. They planned their operations well, believing in the old Ranger adage, "Go off half-cocked and end up whole-dead."

No, it wasn't the prospect of being killed or wounded that was causing him to be uneasy. And forcing him to lose sleep at night. It was something else.

Something he couldn't put his finger on.

His mother, God rest her soul, used to have "the dreams."

That was what she called them, only she'd say the words in an ominous voice, as though her dreams were scary and perhaps evil.

What she termed "the dreams" were her premonitions. They frequently came to her either in the dead of night, forcing her into the kitchen to drink cup after cup of coffee. Just so she wouldn't have to return to bed and risk having another.

Or they'd occur during daydreams, causing her to freak out. Randy remembered once when she'd had a daydream while on her way to drop him off at school.

Into her mind popped a vision – nothing specific - that something dreadful was to happen at school that day. She couldn't say exactly why, but she saw the need to wheel the car around and to return home. Instead of going to school that day he got the day off.

It was okay with him. He spent the day reading "Who'll Catch the Rainbow," a novel about World War II and its effect on the home front.

It wasn't until that evening, when they watched the local news together, that they learned of the out-of-control big rig which had crashed into the wall of the school.

Two were killed, and several were sent to the hospital.

But not Randy. Randy was protected by his mother's premonition.

In fact, his mother's premonitions frequently came true. Not always. But often enough to get the attention of everyone in the family when she had one.

When she got up in the morning to tell of "the dream" she had, plans were changed or canceled outright. Sometimes she didn't leave the house for days, until she decided the danger had passed, or her prediction proved itself true. Once, she was convinced she would fall at work and break her back. She quit without notice. Her husband's insistence that she was being foolish was met with her counterargument, of which she was completely convinced: "The only reason I didn't fall is because I never went back. That proves the dream was correct."

Randy seemed to inherit some of his mother's ability to see danger. Growing up, he sometimes told his friends and teachers to be careful.

"Why?" they'd ask.

"Because I have a feeling something is going to happen to you soon. Something bad."

None of his friends or teachers ever died, but several of them suffered accidents or mishaps, usually within a couple of days of Randy's warnings. Some took his premonitions seriously, but most others scoffed. He learned after awhile to keep his warnings to himself, except for his closest friends. They were the ones most likely to believe him anyway.

He'd had a gnawing feeling in his gut for several days now. It wasn't specific. He couldn't pinpoint it to a specific person, or even an event.

He just felt that something ominous was on the horizon.

Meanwhile, ninety one million miles away, a massive solar storm was brewing on the surface of the sun. That in itself wasn't unusual. The sun was always stormy. But the broiling gasses swirling and competing for space was more massive now than at any other time in two hundred years. It was getting quite ugly on old Sol's mighty face.

Chapter 15

The motel clerk had looked at Randy funny when he requested a wake-up call at three a.m.

"Are you sure?" he'd asked.

"Yes," Randy said while nodding his head. "I'm an early riser."

The truth was, Randy only rose early when he had to. And since he hadn't slept well lately, he half expected to be awake when the phone rang anyway. Probably staring at the ceiling and thinking about his mom and her dreams.

That wasn't the case.

The body has a way of playing catch-up and seems to keep track of the deficit a sleepless person is running. Occasionally it will overrule the stress or whatever is causing sleepless nights and force a body into a good night's sleep, whether one wants it or not.

That was the case on this particular night. Randy slept like a rock.

At least until the phone rang at promptly three a.m.

Randy had fallen asleep as soon as his head hit the pillow. He could barely remember going to bed.

He wanted to roll back over and go back to sleep. But duty was calling, and Randy wasn't the type of man to shirk his responsibilities.

Especially when sleeping in would mean missing the chance to plant long-range surveillance cameras under the cover of darkness. And if they failed to do it now, and missed something important, it could jeopardize their entire case.

He swung around and put two feet on the floor, then forced himself to stand and went in to take a quick shower.

He knew a surefire way to wake himself up.

It wasn't pleasant, but it worked better than coffee or anything else he'd ever tried.

He stepped into the shower and adjusted the water temperature. Hot. Just the way he liked it. He could stand there for hours, until the hot water ran out or his entire body turned into a big pink raisin.

But he had a job to do.

So he turned the hot water completely off and forced himself to stand beneath the frigid water for five straight minutes. By the time he was finished he was no longer in danger of turning into a raisin. His body was shriveled, goose-bumped and shivering.

But he was wide awake.

He turned off the water and dried off, shaved and dressed.

There was a light tap on the door. Three knocks, a pause, and then two.

It was Tom's knock. There was nothing in academy training that said partners on assignment should develop their own special knock. Nothing in the Ranger handbook either. Nothing in the myriad of regulations that covered everything from what type of socks to wear on duty to how many inches their heels should be from their toes while marching in drills.

They'd never discussed the knock between themselves either. Tom just had a very distinctive knock; Randy learned to copy it. That way they knew who was at the door without having to announce it.

It had never come in handy before. It had never saved either of their lives or prevented an ambush. And in all probability it never would. It was just one way among many they'd adapted their behaviors since they'd become partners.

Randy opened the door with his left hand while brushing his teeth with his right, then held up three fingers to indicate to Tom how many minutes before he was ready.

Like an old married couple who could read each other's minds and finish each other's sentences, no more communication was necessary. Tom knew exactly what the three fingers meant.

After Randy rinsed his mouth he sat on the edge of the bed and said, "I'm hungry. Did you see anyplace that might be open this time of morning?"

"I'm way ahead of you partner. I already called the IHOP and ordered two cheeseburgers to go. One fry and one onion ring. Take your pick. I'm not choosy. That's why I have you for a partner."

"Nope. You have me for a partner because I'm tall, dark and handsome. I make our female witnesses swoon and tell me everything we need to know. That's why we solve all of our cases."

"Funny. I though we solved all our cases because I was incredibly smart."

"Yeah, well… you keep telling yourself that if it makes you feel better. Did you order coffee also?"

"Two steaming cups, mine black and yours sissified."

"Atta boy."

An hour later Randy was halfway up a power pole directly across Highway 87 from the ranch. They'd parked their vehicle half a mile away, had worn dark clothing, and had hiked to the pole. Only an occasional oncoming truck cast light in their direction, and Tom was able to hit the dirt each time. When Randy was up on the pole, he was almost invisible. Truck headlights were generally aimed at the pavement in front of it, not up in the air.

Randy mounted two surveillance cameras. They were high tech, the latest thing. Light-enhancing night vision capability, high definition, auto-focus, with tiny solar panels atop each camera to charge the batteries during the day, so they could continue to record all night. These would run nonstop for a maximum of eight days before the memory cards had to be pulled and either purged of data or replaced.

Randy aimed one at the ranch house and zoomed in close. He could easily make out the word "welcome" on the mat in front of the door.

This camera would hopefully capture the faces of everyone who came and went from the house, provided they entered or exited through the front door.

The second camera would record traffic on Farm to Market Road 1348. Randy pressed the "zoom" button until it focused on the exact place where FM 1348 connected with Highway 87. There was a stop sign there, and all vehicles registered in the State of Texas were required to have front plates.

Unless the license plate was intentionally obscured, the camera would record it, as well as the date and time it entered and left the property.

Randy climbed down the pole and said, "Ready. How long until sunrise?"

Tom checked his watch.

"About an hour. Want to take up a position a couple of miles up the road and see if we can catch the Silverado when it goes on the move?"

"Sounds like a plan. Count me in."

Chapter 16

For much of the morning, the Chevy truck led the Rangers on a laundry list of errands. First to the convenience store next to Janice's diner, where the driver of the pickup seemed to take quite a fascination in scratch-off lottery tickets.

Three times he entered the store, walking up to the cash register and pointing to various tickets behind the counter, having the cashier tear off each ticket and then ring up his total.

While the cashier had his back turned, one of the driver's friends walked casually up and down the aisles, occasionally stuffing things into the sleeves of a bulky coat and into his pockets.

Tom, watching from afar with the Bushnells, counted two cans of beer, a box of wet-wipes, a tube of toothpaste and a box of Pop-Tarts.

"Well," observed Tom, "If we don't get them for drug trafficking we've got them for shoplifting."

"Don't forget organized crime."

"Good point."

Tacking on organized crime charges to relatively small offenses was a growing practice among Texas and federal prosecutors. It was first tried in Houston several years before to gain control over street gangs which were running rampant across the city and causing mass chaos.

A smart prosecutor said, "Hey, we have these three burglars who were caught burglarizing a business together. Individually we can give each of them two to three years in state prison.

"However, if we can give one of them immunity to admit they were working together to get money to score a large amount of drugs to resell, then that comes under the organized crime statute. That's an additional five to ten for the two who didn't get immunity. And eventually they'll use street justice to take care of the guy who rolled on them."

The tactic worked remarkably well. Word got around, and now prosecutors all over Texas were using similar tactics to send people away for relatively minor offenses.

It was their way of saying, "so there" to parole boards who kept turning repeat offenders back onto the streets.

From the convenience store the Chevy went to a dry cleaning establishment, where one of the flunkies in the back got out and retrieved a handful of suits. Probably for the boss, probably Mexican made, probably tailored.

Randy made a mental note to return to the cleaners later and to try to get some information from the proprietors. Like, for example, the cell phone number the mysterious men left should something happen to their dry cleaning.

After the cleaners the truck pulled up to a gas station, where the driver used a credit card to fill the tank.

Randy made an entry in his notebook as to the date and time, the name of the station and the intersection. He'd have to get a court order to get it, but the credit card information would be useful. If the name on the card could be traced back to a particular cartel, it would tell them who was bankrolling the operation.

Next stop was back to Janice's diner.

The Rangers opted out of a visit themselves, though. Being there two days in a row at the same time as their suspects would appear to be suspicious if the suspects were paying attention at all. And one thing both men had learned at the Ranger Academy: always assume you're being watched as closely as the suspects you're surveilling.

Frequently when surveillance teams are made, the suspects carry on as though they aren't aware.

Sometimes they do it to mess with the cops' heads. They become boy scouts and are careful not to conduct any criminal activity at all. They're careful not to even jaywalk or run any stop signs. Their intent is to waste the cops' time and frustrate them into abandoning their surveillance and moving on to something more fruitful.

Other times, the bad guys aren't sure who it is that's watching them. The logical assumption is that it's law enforcement. But that's not always the case. Frequently they don't let on that the surveillance is blown, and conduct their own covert operations to make sure it's not a rival gang or cartel trying to take over their operation.

Or some misguided group of thugs looking to steal their dope.

Chapter 17

Randy and Tom had just turned off the ignition key after parking their pickup a full two blocks from the diner.

Both of the eased back their seats and reclined them, trying to get comfortable for what they expected was at least half an hour's wait.

Luckily Tom was paying attention.

"Oh, crap. They're on the move again."

He raised the high-powered binoculars back up to his eyes and focused them in on the Silverado, which had pulled out of the diner's lot and was heading directly for them.

Randy restarted the truck quickly and pulled away from the curb, then took an immediate right onto a residential street. He drove the speed limit, not wanting to look out of place or in a hurry, until he saw the suspect vehicle drive past in his rear view mirror.

Then he doubled back, again in no hurry.

By the time he got back to the place where he'd parked his truck, the Silverado was but a tiny dot in the distance. It hadn't changed course, hadn't doubled back, hadn't pulled over to see if it was being followed.

"What do you think?" Randy asked. "Think they made us?"

"Nope. They had to go one way or the other. Chances were fifty-fifty they'd come toward us. I think we're still cool."

As it turned out, the driver only stayed in the parking lot of the diner long enough to run in for a cup of coffee and to drop off his companions. Now he was riding solo and on a mission.

The Rangers had no way of knowing that. For all they knew, the vehicle was still full of armed thugs, and they were still outnumbered. It was still imperative they keep their distance.

The Silverado took a slow and deliberate path to an empty parking lot outside a football stadium.

It was the only such stadium in town and belonged to the local school district.

A billboard sized sign hung over the entry to the lot, proclaiming:

WELCOME TO BOBCAT STADIUM
HOME OF BELTON HIGH SCHOOL
DIVISION 2-AA STATE CHAMPIONS
1980 1985 1991

The sign was painted on a white background with dark blue letters, the school colors of Belton High. Once a football powerhouse, the school's glory days were behind her.

The sign, like the team, had seen its best days. The paint was peeling now and fading in the sunlight. Yet it still shined as a beacon of pride, and of hope, each Friday night in the fall when the stadium lights came on.

On this particular morning, though, it served only to mark a meeting place.

Randy and Tom sensed something was up as they parked in front of a boarded-up convenience store two blocks away.

Tom reached into the console and took out a Nikon digital camera. From under the seat he pulled out a telephoto lens in a soft zippered case.

He connected the two and zoomed in on his target.

Randy looked in his driver's side mirror and said, "Cop."

Both hunkered down in their seats for several seconds as a white police car came up behind them and passed them by.

The single man inside the car didn't even glance in their direction. Even if he had, he likely wouldn't have noticed the tops of their heads through the heavily tinted windows.

Randy snuck a peek over the steering wheel and didn't sound the all clear until the patrol car was more than a block away and still maintaining its speed.

Tom raised up and focused the camera on the back of the patrol car, specifically the license plate, and snapped four photos in rapid succession.

He asked Randy, "Did you get a look at him?"

"Only in my mirror, and from half a block away. One occupant, Caucasian male, middle aged."

"Could be the chief."

"Maybe. Let's see where he goes."

They watched as the patrol car entered the parking lot of the stadium and pulled alongside the Chevy Silverado, facing toward them. Randy couldn't see beans from that distance. So Tom, watching through the telephoto lens as he snapped photo after photo, provided the play-by-play.

"The man in the patrol car is indeed our chief. And they appear to know one another. Either that or he's the friendliest guy around. He's got a grin on his face like the Cheshire cat."

"Any idea what they're talking about?"

"Nope. I should have signed up for that optional lip reading class at the Academy. It looks like they're just two buddies on a fishing trip."

"Can you get a good look at our Silverado driver?"

"Nope. He's pointing in the wrong direction and his mirrors are at the wrong angle. Uh, oh…"

"Uh, oh what? That's never a good sign."

"They're exchanging something."

"Any idea?"

"Nope. Looks like a manila envelope. Too thin to be a package of dope. We can enlarge the photos later and maybe get a better idea."

"I sure wish we had audio."

"Yeah. Me too. You think we have enough probable cause to get a judge to sign off on that?"

"I'd say it depends on who's in the pickup. If he's a known felon, and they met on cordial terms and exchanged something between them, I'd say the odds are in our favor."

"Yeah. I think so too."

They continued to watch as the patrol car pulled out of the stadium parking lot and went in the opposite direction, away from them.

"Your choice. Tail the chief or tail the truck?"

"Let's go with the truck. We know who the chief is. Let's see if we can get an ID on the other guy."

Chapter 18

Next stop for the Silverado was at a self-storage facility, the only one in Belton.

It was, according to the information packet they'd received when being assigned the case, owned by the police chief's brother.

"The plot thickens," Tom said as he saw the vehicle pull into the facility's yard, then disappear through a pass-coded security gate.

The facility was surrounded by a six foot privacy fence on all sides. But the Chevy truck had been raised, and its top could be seen over the top of the fence as it drove around the perimeter of the compound to a building on the far corner of the property.

Tom, looking through the binoculars, said, "Make a note of this. I can't see the number on the unit, but it's the second one from the west end in the very last building."

"We'll come back later and peek over the fence and get a look at the number. We may need it for a search warrant later. And I'm guessing we won't get a lot of cooperation from the owner if we show up and flash a badge and ask what the number on that particular unit was."

"Right. He'd likely give us a phony number, and then clean the place out as soon as we were out of sight."

"And then tell his brother we were here snooping around. That's the trouble with operations in these small towns. We're given the basic information, as far as who the players are. But it doesn't go very deep. For all we know, our waitress friend Janice could be the cousin of the chief."

"Yeah. Or his girlfriend. What I don't like about small town operations is that everybody knows everybody else. And that makes it harder for us to blend in, or even get around, without being looked at with suspicion. We may as well tow a billboard behind us that says, 'nosy strangers' on it."

"Here he comes."

They watched as the top of the Silverado traversed the perimeter of the property again, retracing its earlier path.

The truck came back into view at the wrought iron gate. As the driver leaned out to punch a code into the gate's keypad Randy used the telephoto lens on his Nikon to snap a fairly good phot of the man's face.

"That should help in the ID process."

One of the really cool features the State of Texas added during the previous SLEN upgrade was facial recognition software. It still had a lot of bugs in it, and wasn't the most reliable program, but it was in its infancy and would someday be a very effective tool for the state's law enforcement agencies.

Randy was hoping they got lucky and that this was one of the faces the program would recognize.

As their prey pulled away, Tom called out, "There appears to be a bunch of stuff in the back of the truck now."

"What does it look like?"

"Don't know. It's all covered with a tarp. Damn it!"

He looked sheepishly at Randy, when he remembered Randy had a severe dislike for the word.

"I mean *darn it*. 'Darn it's' what I meant to say."

As they followed the truck back to the town proper Tom's curiosity got the best of him.

"Randy, I've been meaning to ask. I know you don't like it when people use words like 'damn' and 'hell.' And you're right. I use them way too much. But why is it you don't like them, exactly?"

"I don't rightly know. I guess because I never heard my parents use them when I was growing up. I'd hear my dad accidentally bang his thumb with a hammer and he'd say something like 'dad-gummit' or 'good gosh.'

I'd be at my friends' houses and hear their parents say the words you said and much worse. And I guess that somewhere along the line I just decided that my dad's way of dealing with life's unpleasant surprises was just… classier, I guess. For lack of a better word.

"My mom used to say that cursing was a way for the less intelligent or less well-read to express their feelings. I'm not sure I agree with her on that. I mean, I've known some pretty smart people in my life. And many of them cursed. So that may be true for some people but not others.

"I guess it's out of respect for my dad, more than anything. He was the greatest man I've known in my entire life. And he didn't curse. So I guess in my own mind I've linked the two qualities together. The not cursing and the deserving of great respect. I suppose that's why."

"Did you know that some of the other Rangers consider you preachy?"

"I know. I've been told that. And I always apologize. I don't mean to be. I mean, I sometimes ask people not to use that kind of language around me, but I'm not overbearing about it. I usually make the request and if they choose to disregard it I just try as best as I can to ignore their words. But if they ask me why, I tell them the truth. That those words are unnecessary, and I have much more respect for someone who can communicate his or her feelings without being uncivil."

"Okay, fair enough. Like I said, I use that kind of language far too often and should cut back on it anyway. My son Jacob, he's five now. He said the 'f-word' the other day after he jumped off the couch and turned his ankle. Sandra snapped him up and demanded to know where he'd heard that word. He said, 'Daddy says it in the car sometimes, when he yells it at other drivers.'

"Sandra looked at me and didn't say anything. But she didn't have to. I need to learn to watch my language for my kid's sake. So I can practice by watching it around you."

"Thank you, Tom. That would mean a lot to me. And I'm not trying to change you as a person. I'm really not. I just don't like those words, in the same way some people don't like broccoli."

"Okay then, my friend. I'll make a deal with you. I hate broccoli with a passion. I'll try not to use offensive language around you if you try never to eat broccoli around me. Fair enough?"

Randy laughed his easy laugh. The one who made him a genuinely likeable guy to practically everyone he ever met.

"Okay, partner. It's a deal."

Chapter 19

The Silverado left the storage facility and followed a now-familiar track back to the diner.

From a quarter mile away the Rangers kept it in view while they waited for the driver to rejoin his friends. To pass the time they talked of the television shows they watched growing up.

"My favorite shows were *Hawaii Five-O* and *The Rockford Files*," Randy offered. "Lots of action in both of them. The characters were likeable, and the good guys always won."

"I watched mostly science fiction," Tom replied. "The crime shows were okay back then, I guess. But even when I was a kid I could tell they weren't very realistic."

"How so?"

"Well, there was never any blood, for one thing. When the bad guy got shot, he didn't bleed. I've seen guys get shot for real, and it can be a pretty bloody mess. And when they fight, the bad guy usually goes out with one punch. Out like a light. When I was in my first barroom brawl, I was under the mistaken impression that all I had to do was hit the guy one time. And then he'd go to the floor unconscious and I could go back and finish my beer."

Randy smiled. He suspected he knew the answer to his question, but asked it anyway.

"So I take it he didn't go down?"

"The guy was bigger than a tank. He was harassing the waitress, and I was just drunk enough to think if I rescued her she'd go home with me and call me her hero. So I told the guy to stop or else.

"He stood in front of me and said, 'Or else what?'

"So I belted him. Like I said, I expected him to fall right to the floor. But it didn't even phase him. He smiled. Then he kicked my ass."

"That doesn't sound much like a barroom brawl."

"Oh, it was. My friends tried to save me from my own stupidity. His friends came to battle my friends. In the end there were like, seven of us who got thrown out of the bar.

"The waitress came outside to talk to me."

"Really? Was she grateful?"

"She called me a sap. It turned out the big guy was her boyfriend. She went home with him and called *him* her hero, not me. I learned a lot about human nature that day."

"I hope you also learned not to start a fight in a bar."

"Yeah, that too."

"You know something else that wasn't realistic in the old TV shows?"

"What?"

"The way they did things. For example, if this were a TV show, and you and I were the detectives, we'd go over to the diner to see what was in the back of that pickup, underneath that tarp. You would distract the bad guys by going inside the diner and talking some nonsensical trash to them. And I'd go to the back of the pickup and lift up the tarp to see what was underneath it."

"Right. And there would be no judge who'd throw the evidence out as illegally obtained. No lawyer claiming his client was railroaded, no news reporters sticking microphones in our faces and demanding to know why we thought we were above the law."

"Yeah. The shows were entertaining but not very realistic."

"That's because if they showed police work as it really was, nobody would watch. I mean, who'd watch a show where two guys sat in a car for hours at a time drinking cold coffee and talking about the 1970 Pittsburgh Steelers?"

"Probably nobody. At least those old TV shows had some really cool police chases."

"Yeah. Did you notice that all the cars they wrecked were old beat up junkers? They never wrecked the newer cars. It wasn't in their budget. And they always showed the wrecks from different angles, so they could get more footage by showing the same wrecks several different times. And they slowed them down a little, just enough to stretch the footage a little bit more."

"Those old shows were still better than a lot of the stuff they show on TV these days."

"No doubt. Hey, they're loading up."

Tom watched through his binoculars as the Silverado driver emerged from the diner. The men he'd dropped off earlier followed him out and trailed him to the pickup in a single file. They reminded Tom of ducklings following their mother.

Only these ducklings weren't harmless. They were probably well armed, and probably vicious. The Mexican cartels didn't allow their men to come to the United States and operate out of their sight unless they'd proven their mettle.

And could be trusted to fight for the cartel if called upon to.

The suspects drove up Highway 87 to their now-familiar cutoff to FM Road 1348 and exited as they had before. Randy drove past, continuing several miles north toward Amarillo before making a U-turn and heading back.

They hoped to find the men unloading whatever was on the back of the pickup as they passed by the ranch house, and Randy slowed as they grew close.

Not slow enough to be conspicuous. But slow enough to maybe get a peek.

Tom had the camera out and focused on the Silverado as they drove past, shooting one photo rapidly after another.

But there wasn't much to see. The tarp was still on the back of the truck, covering whatever secret cargo lay beneath it.

"Must be something good," Randy observed. "They're going to wait until after dark to unload it."

"How much battery life do we have on the long range cameras?"

"At least three days."

"Good. We'll let them do the work. Let's go to Lubbock and get in some computer time."

Chapter 21

Tom poured their coffee while Randy sat at his desk and logged onto SLEN. He dutifully poured two packets of non-dairy creamer and two packets of sugar into his partner's coffee while asking, "When are you going to start drinking your coffee like a real Ranger, Randy?"

"I don't know, Tom. How does a real Ranger drink his coffee?"

"Well, for example, like your great great grandfather did. On the range, while he was dodging Comanche arrows. He heated up a pot of coffee on the campfire and drank it still boiling, as black as the devil's heart."

Randy didn't skip a beat.

"Actually, family legend has it that old Wilford P. never drank coffee. Said it made him too jumpy. It was said he had a shot of whisky before each trail ride, and another to celebrate his safe return."

"Interesting. Maybe we should do that."

"Suit yourself. But you know I don't drink."

"I know, Randy. I'm just messing with you. Besides, I'd never drink on duty. That's asking for trouble, and I've got a feeling those hombres we're trailing are trouble enough as it is."

"I'm afraid you're right. And back to the coffee thing. I have sugar in my coffee because it takes a lot to maintain my level of sweetness. And the ladies seem to like it."

"Like what?"

"My level of sweetness."

"Okay. If you say so. Anything on SLEN?"

"It's coming up now."

The facial recognition software in SLEN was new and still unreliable. As such, it was hit-and-miss. Randy loaded the long-range photo they'd taken of the pick-up's driver as a .jpg file and hit "enter."

An hourglass appeared in the center of the screen and slowly rotated once, twice, three times.

Then a pop-up replaced the hourglass.

A pop-up that said, "Match not found."

Randy was disappointed, but not surprised.

"Let's run the plate," Tom suggested.

Randy looked at another photograph and punched a few more keys.

The license plate came back to a Julio Castro, with an address in Odessa. Odessa was a couple of hours south of Lubbock, and a lot closer to Mexico.

"Interesting. Maybe Mr. Castro is our Mexican connection."

"Maybe. Or maybe this network stretches far beyond Belton and Lubbock. Maybe they're supplying drugs for the Midland and Odessa area as well."

Randy punched a few more keys and a year-old mugshot of Julio Castro appeared on the screen.

"Uh, oh…"

Randy read Castro's rap sheet beneath the photo.

It was extensive, dating back for almost twenty years. It included two stints in TDCJ, or the Texas Department of Criminal Justice.

The Texas prison system.

The latest charge, the one which generated the mugshot, was a felony one charge. Manufacture of methamphetamine. And possession of two hundred grams of the junk with intent to distribute it.

The line that ran across the top of the mugshot announced that a fugitive warrant had been issued by a federal judge in Dallas.

Mr. Castro was on the run.

"Why would they even give this guy bail?" Randy asked. This one would have sent him away for twenty years of hard time, no chance of parole for fifteen. And he's got ties to Mexico. They didn't think he'd run?"

"Judges are idiots, Randy. Too many of them are soft-hearted and soft-headed. And a lot of them think the best way to solve the problem is just to send these guys running back to Mexico instead of spending the time and resources prosecuting them. So they grant bonds knowing that number one, the money is there to cover the bond. And two, we'll never see this particular guy again. At least not on American soil. Problem solved. At least in their eyes."

"Yeah. And that may solve the short term problem. But all this guy does is to pass his operation to the next guy in line."

"And there's *always* somebody else next in line."

"Meanwhile, the junk they're bringing in is killing this country in so many ways. People looking to escape their poverty or pain turn to these drugs to feel better. They get hooked and lives are destroyed. They hurt their family and loved ones, then their friends. They steal from everybody they know until everyone disowns them. Then they steal from strangers until they get locked up.

"After they get out, they're in the same position they were in before. They're still broke and still hurt. Only now they have no more family and no more friends. And a prison record. And the bleeding hearts wonder why so damn many of them go right back into doing drugs and stealing again."

Randy just looked at him.

Tom shrugged his shoulders and said, "Hey, I know I get passionate about this whole thing. I've got family members who were in the game. I've seen the damage it can do. It's almost a lost cause."

"Maybe. But we can't give up. The only way to keep them from winning is to keep plugging away. Keep winning the little battles in the hopes we can someday win the war."

"Yep. Okay, partner. I'll get off my high horse now. I know I've been preaching to the choir. So where do we go from here?"

"Well, the guy in the mugshot definitely wasn't the driver of the Silverado. We'll print it out and keep it. It may come in handy if he's one of the ones who thinks he's invincible enough to stay in the area. Then we lay low for a couple of days. We don't want to spend so much time in Belton that people start recognizing us. We'll sneak back tomorrow night and check out our video. See what was in the back of that pickup truck. Then we'll have a better idea of what we're dealing with."

Chapter 22

When Randy pulled up in front of Tom's place the next morning, Tom was sitting on his front steps reading a book.

He had a smile on his face. Randy was surprised, because he knew darn well that Tom wasn't looking forward to the task ahead of him on this particular morning.

Some traditions died hard.

The Texas Rangers started out on horseback. It was in their blood. And now, some 180 years after the first group of Texas lawmen were issued their now-famous five pointed stars, it was still an agency tradition.

The Ranger handbook still extolled the virtues of being able to "ride hard and fast."

"Texas is still chock full of open range," the handbook stated. "Much of it is inaccessible by vehicle. Ranger operations frequently extend onto these lands, and it is therefore a valuable asset for our officers to hone his or her skills as a horseman. Riding skills are but one of the tools that make a successful Ranger. And it furthers the heritage which made our organization great."

Despite the heavy-handed suggestions from day one of training that recruits gain a proficiency in riding it was technically no longer required.

But it might as well have been.

For many off-duty activities Rangers were involved in took place in ranch settings, or involved ranching skills. Friendly riding competitions. Retirement parties on the ranches of retired Rangers who roasted a side of beef on a spit while active duty Rangers wrestled steers or raced their ponies in the background.

It was standard practice for Rangers to get together when off-duty and go to the rodeo whenever it was in town.

Yes, horseback riding was in the blood of the Texas Rangers.

It was not unlike retired athletes who got together on weekends and organized flag football games or three on three basketball games.

Major Shultz was distressed to learn, upon Tom Cohen's assignment to Lubbock's Company C, that he still hadn't taken the initiative to learn to ride.

"Well, it's against regulations for me to withhold your promotion to sergeant based simply upon your inability to ride a horse," he'd said. "And the regulations prohibit me from giving you a bad rating on your annual performance report for that same reason."

He'd glared across his expansive desk at the young Ranger and spoke slowly, as though he wanted each word to sink in and take hold.

"But mark my words, young fella. You'll never be a *true* Ranger until you learn how to ride. The regulations don't say I can't post you wherever I want when we have an operation on horseback. So from here on out, whenever we're on horseback, I'm gonna put you on the orneriest and meanest stallion in our stables. You'll either learn how to ride or you'll spend a lot of time climbing back on him after getting bucked off."

Randy's showing up to Company C not long after provided a remedy to the problem.

Randy had been riding almost as long as he'd been walking. He could handle a horse as well as any man in the region, and had worked part time at a ranch while still in high school.

"I have an additional assignment for you," the major had told Randy. This one is not official, and I don't expect to see any mention to it on any time sheets or reports. This one will last until I say to stop. It may be an assignment that lasts three months. It may last three years. The length of time on this one depends on how good a teacher you are."

Randy had been confused.

"Teacher?"

"Yes. Twice a month until I say otherwise, I want you to spend half a day teaching your partner how to ride. Nothing fancy. I don't need for him to be able to shoot a silver dollar out of the air at a full gallop. All I need is for him to get from point A to point B at a fast clip without falling off his damn horse."

Randy had tried hard to stifle a smile.

But the major wasn't kidding.

"We can't have a greenhorn in our ranks, Randy. It's embarrassing." We're the God-forsaken Texas Rangers, for crying out loud. Our proud heritage depends on this."

Tom was still smiling when he opened the cab of Randy's truck and climbed in.

Randy asked, "What's so funny, tenderfoot?"

"I just found out that John Wayne hated horses."

It was like a punch in the gut to Randy, who grew up adoring the big cowboy and loving every one of his movies.

"What? What are you talking about, Tom?"

"It's right here, in this book."

Tom handed Randy a soft-covered book.

Randy examined the cover.

1001 Little Known Things about Well Known People, by Charlie Bennett.

Tom reached over and took back the book, then turned it to a particular page. He read aloud.

"John Wayne, the most recognized American cowboy actor around the world, despised horses. 'They are filthy and disgusting creatures,' he once said. He only tolerated them because making his movies without them would have been impossible."

Tom looked at his partner and said, "See? It's not just me. John Wayne hated horses too."

"Where'd you get that book?"

"On Amazon."

"Well, I'll be darned. I never knew that about the Duke."

"Do you know where he got that nickname? *The Duke?*"

"No."

"From his dog. He hung out at a fire station when he was a boy. The firemen used to tease him that he always had the same downtrodden expression as his dog. His dog's name was Duke, so they started calling him Duke too."

"I'll be darned. I always figured he was given the title by some English queen or something."

"Did you know that in some of his early movies they put him on a horse that was way too small for him, to make him appear bigger than life?"

"I've got one for you, Tom. What was one thing John Wayne could do that you couldn't?"

"I don't know, Randy. What?"

"Ride a horse. Put the book down and let's go fix that."

Chapter 23

Randy exuded a quiet confidence in the saddle. He'd had the horse, a tall Morgan named Trigger, for several years before he applied to the Ranger Academy. They were old friends.

Trigger seemed able to read Randy's mind. They moved in a fluid motion, the big horse almost anticipating each pull of the reins.

They were as one.

Tom and his loaner horse Buddy, not so much.

Randy reminded him of an earlier lesson before he got on.

"You complained about saddle sores after your last session. Try to relax. Try not to bounce as much in the saddle. Relax your legs and resist the urge to squeeze them tight against the saddle. Just relax and go with the flow. Lean toward the pony when he runs. When you turn him, lean into the turns a bit too."

"I did that once last time and fell off."

"I said lean, not lay down. The point is, the horse will do the driving. Let him. Just as you have to train him to get used to you, you have to train yourself to get used to him. You have to learn to relax in the saddle and not worry about you're doing. Before long you'll be used to each other and you'll have a much more comfortable ride."

"More comfortable ride… does that mean no more blisters on my ass?"

"Yes. That's exactly what it means. As soon as you learn to relax and stop bouncing around like a bobble head in the saddle."

Before they put the gear on the horse's back Randy had him greet the horse with a smile.

"Rub him behind his ears. Talk nice to him. Horses are smart. Most of them are smarter than most humans you know. They can sense whether you are a friend or a foe, and they'll treat their friends much nicer. Most of them, like Buddy here, can recognize a tenderfoot like yourself a mile away. He'll be gentle and patient with you, but only if you deserve it. You have to convince him you're not a jerk. That you're a nice guy who's not here to hurt him. But rather here to be his friend and work with him."

"Oh, great. Now I not only have to ride him, but I have to be his pal too."

"Well, you don't have to be. But remember that he's a lot bigger than you. And it's totally within his discretion whether to give you a pleasant ride today or to take off with you through the mesquite brush. So if you're smart you'll let him know you're willing to be his friend."

"And just how the hell do I do that?"

"There's that word again. Remember what I told you last time. Walk up to him from the front. Don't surprise him. Talk to him as you would a friend. Let him become familiar with your voice. Pat him on the shoulder. Rest your hand there. Let him become familiar with your touch. Call him by name. Ask him how he's doing. Scratch him behind the ears. They like that. Mention the word apple a lot."

"Yeah. You said that last time. Tell me again why I have to mention apple a lot."

"Because he recognizes the word and knows it's his reward for a job well done. It'll give him something to look forward to at the end of your ride. And he'll be on his best behavior so he can earn that apple."

Tom reached behind Buddy's ear and began to scratch as instructed.

The big horse suddenly drew back with a huff. Then he lifted his front leg and came down hard, his hoof scraping the side of Tom's boot.

"What the?"

Tom drew back in fear.

Randy took the lead from Tom's hands and talked gently to the horse to calm him down.

"Hey, hey, what's the matter, big fella?" he asked as he held the lead tight and rubbed the horse's long nose.

Once Buddy was calm he inspected the area behind his ear.

"That's why he jerked. He's got a sore back there. Looks like something bit him and he's got an infection. Wait here."

Tom said, "Well, I damn sure ain't gonna get on him and ride off, after he just tried to kill me."

Randy chuckled and disappeared into the tack room.

He emerged a minute later still chuckling.

"Okay, drama queen. Were you hurt? Did he violate your sensitivities?"

"No. But he brushed against the side of my boot."

"Listen, Tom. If he wanted to hurt you, you'd be hopping around on one foot now, with the other foot and a couple of toes broken. He knew exactly where your foot was, and he wasn't trying to hurt you. He was sending you a message. You were hurting him and he was telling you to back off."

"I think he was telling me he wanted me dead and he was going to stomp me into the ground."

Randy laughed as he used his fingers to scoop a big dollop of salve from a yellow and red can marked "Corona."

"What's that? I thought Corona was a beer."

"It is. But it's also a salve that's been around for more than a hundred years. It'll soothe him and help his sore heal, and will keep the flies from laying eggs in it."

Buddy saw the familiar can and calmed down.

"See, I told you he was smart. He recognizes the can and equates it to medicine. And I'm guessing he's smart enough to know that you meant him no harm. He won't hold it against you. Will ya, boy?"

Buddy huffed and brushed his oversized head against Randy's shoulder.

Randy said, "See? He says he didn't mean to scare you."

"I still don't think I can trust him enough to get on him today. Let's come back another day."

"Tom, you can't be a sissy all your life. Let's get them saddled up. You can ride Trigger and I'll take Buddy out. Now hike up your skirt and grab those saddle blankets over there."

Chapter 24

The ride went off without a hitch, and Trigger sensed he had a tenderfoot upon his back.

As they removed the saddles and prepared to brush down the horses, Tom remarked, "You know, this wasn't so bad today. If I could ride Trigger all the time I think I might actually enjoy this."

"Don't even try it," Randy countered. "I don't mind you riding him a couple of more times, if it'll help you get comfortable in the saddle. But Trigger is more to me than just a horse. He's more like a great friend. We're a team, him and I. And he's way more loyal to me than most of the humans I've come across."

"Randy, I get the impression you were born in the wrong place and time."

"What do you mean?"

"Well, you come across as somebody from an old western movie. Kind of an 'aw shucks, ma'am' kind of guy who's equal parts Gomer Pyle, Beaver Cleaver and John Wayne. You don't smoke, drink or cuss, and you make a point to go to church every Sunday. Are you that way for real, or are you just putting on a show to catch a girl?"

Randy pondered his partner's question, not really knowing how to take it. It was possible Tom was making fun of him and his gentle nature. But he didn't think so. He seemed to be genuinely curious.

"I don't know how to answer that, Tom. I don't consider myself any different than anyone else. Maybe I've got fewer bad habits than some, but bad habits don't make someone a bad person. I guess I was just raised differently than most folks."

"How so?"

"Well, my earliest recollections of my grandfather were those of a tall man, opening doors for others and tipping his hat to strangers on the street. He didn't smoke or cuss or drink either, and I guess that's the example he set for my father. And my father on to me, I guess. My father was just like him in every respect, except that he didn't tip his hat because he seldom wore a hat after he retired from the Rangers. Said they made his head sweat."

"Do you think it was that... being the son and grandson of Rangers, that made you as pure as you are?"

Randy chuckled again.

"Well, I don't know if *pure* is the word I'd use. My mom used to say I was born into the wrong era. That I'd have fit right into the late 18th century, when women were revered and men were gentlemen because they were raised that way, not because they felt they had to be. What you see is what I am. I don't put on airs or pretend to be anything I'm not. Like me or not, that's the way I've always lived my life."

"And does that work?"

"What do you mean, does it work?"

"Does it work to pick up girls?"

Randy laughed out loud.

"You're not hearing me, Tom. I'm not the way I am to pick up girls. I don't have any trouble finding them. They seem to find me. But I don't intentionally act the way I do to attract them. Women long for the good old days, I think, when men treated them with respect and not as body parts. The truth is, I date often, but I'm honest with them up front. I don't want to get involved in a serious relationship until my ten years as a Ranger are up."

"Why?"

"Because I'm ending the legacy. I'll do my ten years. I owe that much to the Maloneys who wore this badge before I did. But it's just a matter of time before our string of luck runs out. Just a matter of time before one of us is killed in the line of duty. Just a matter of time before the lives of one of our wives or children get shattered. And if I love a woman enough to marry her, then I love her enough to not want to do that to her. So I tell them all, every last one of them, that I'll get married after my time in the Rangers is through. Then I'll settle down and lead a normal life. And I'll bury this badge next to my great great granddad, where it rightfully belongs."

"If you're worried about being killed while wearing the badge, then why wear it at all? Why not end the legacy by not signing onto the Rangers yourself?"

"Because my heroes have always been Rangers. And because when I was four years old I promised my dad I'd wear his badge one day. And that I'd make him proud."

Chapter 25

At just a few minutes past midnight Randy was awakened by a shudder that ran through his apartment in west Lubbock.

This wasn't an unusual occurrence of late.

Randy was born at West Texas Hospital in downtown Lubbock and spent most of his life in the hub city. But he'd never felt an earthquake until a couple of years before.

Environmental activists claimed it was the oil industry, and their newly developed technology which enabled them to squeeze oil from the ground by fracking.

Doomsday believers claimed it was a warning from God Himself, telling man he needed to right his ways and repent.

Randy himself took the earthquakes in stride, as he did most other things.

They were relatively minor, seldom registering more than 2.5 on the Richter scale. Just enough to rattle his dishes a bit and make him go around his apartment the next day, straightening all the pictures on his walls.

And since they were becoming more and more common, there was nothing at all unusual about this particular quake.

What was unusual was the dream that it interrupted.

For Randy was sound asleep just before the quake came rolling through, speaking to his long-dead mother.

About the sun, of all things.

Most people remember only bits and pieces of their dreams. Little snippets of short duration which leave them wondering what in the world their dreams were all about.

Not so Randy.

Randy's dreams were expansive and in full living color. Forget the scientists who claimed that people only dreamed in black and white and mistakenly thought their images were colorful. Randy would argue until his last breath that wasn't true in his case.

His dreams were vivid and memorable. He could frequently describe them in detail even days later, and recite verbatim what was said and by whom.

This particular dream, the one he was shaken out of by the earthquake, was way more disturbing than the quake itself.

Randy had been sitting at the dining room table in his mother's house. The one he'd sold a few years before. He had remarked how beautiful she looked, despite the wrinkles and graying hair that premature aging and the stress of being a Ranger's wife had given her.

Randy didn't dispense false modesty to any woman, and certainly not to his own mother. She'd have seen right through it anyway. She knew that when he said she was beautiful, he really meant it. She was always beautiful in his eyes.

"Thank you, son. I can always count on you to put a smile on my face, even on my worst days. I don't feel beautiful at all, but I'm glad you still see me in that way."

"I don't know any other way to see you, mother."

"I'm here to warn you, son."

"To warn me? About what? Are you sick? Is something going to happen to you?"

"This isn't about me, Randy. My days on this earth are numbered. We both know that, and I'm okay with it. I've accepted that God will call me home soon, and I have but one regret. I regret that I don't have more time to spend with you. But I don't worry about you. Not anymore. You've grown into the finest man I've ever known. And I'm more proud of you than any mother has a right to be. I know you'll thrive and continue to make me proud, every last day of your life."

Randy had felt his face flush, even in the dream. He wasn't a man who took praise well, even when it was being heaped upon him by his own adoring mother.

"Mother, you're embarrassing me."

"I'm sorry, Randy. But darn it, a mother has a right to tell her boy she's proud of the fine and upstanding man he's become."

He deflected the attention away from himself by asking for clarification.

"Then what, mom? If it's not about you then what do you want to warn me about?"

"Randy, you know I've always had the gift."

He knew instantly what she was referring to.

Her premonitions.

Her family had called it, "the gift" amongst themselves. Randy's grandmother had had it. So had her mother and grandfather. The degrees varied from generation to generation, but with each successive generation had come claims of being visionaries or seers, or merely family members whose dreams tended to come true on occasion.

"I know, mother. You know I've had visions myself from time to time."

"It's a heavy cross to bear, my son. Many times you see things which will happen to those you love, good or bad. And frequently to people you know only in passing. You struggle with a decision, whether to share your knowledge with people who will laugh at you and scoff you. Oftentimes you'll keep your secrets to yourself to preserve your own good name. Then you'll feel guilty for not sharing things which might have helped others."

Randy hadn't a clue where she was going, so he chose to let her ramble, offering only a noncommittal, "Yes, ma'am."

"Randy, there's trouble ahead. Big time trouble. Trouble on a scale mankind has never seen before. And it's coming in your lifetime. Not mine, but yours. I'll be gone, and won't be around to help you get through it. The only help I can offer you is a warning. A warning that it's coming. And a plea for you to recognize it and to prepare for it."

Randy could vividly recall the look of terror on his mother's face.

He'd asked, "What, mother? Prepare for what?"

She stroked his face and said tenderly, "That's just it, my son. I don't know exactly what the threat is and I can't understand it, for it makes no sense at all to me. All I know for sure is that it has something to do with the sun."

Chapter 26

Randy rolled over and hugged his pillow while pondering what the dream meant.

He closed his eyes, even knowing it would be impossible to go back to sleep.

Had his mother visited him from beyond the grave, to warn him of a coming catastrophe?

Or was his imagination working overtime?

Instinctively he suspected he knew the answer. And it unnerved him. At least enough to resolve to himself to do some research in the coming days about the sun. And the various ways it could threaten life on earth.

For now, though, he was awake and wasn't likely to go back to sleep anytime soon.

So he might as well get up and look around, to see if his apartment had suffered any cracked walls or other damage from the quake.

And to see if his partner was awake.

In the grand scheme of things, he only lost two hours of sleep. He'd planned to get up at two a.m. anyway. Tom was picking him up at 2:45 for the seventy minute drive to Belton. The plan was to climb up the telephone pole along Highway 87 their surveillance cameras were mounted on and to switch out the memory cards.

He liked Tom. They weren't just partners, they'd become good friends. And they'd been partners and friends long enough to be able to read each other like books.

They knew each other's habits enough to make predictions on what they might do or not do under specific circumstances.

And in this case, when an earthquake woke Randy up from a dead sleep, and almost certainly did the same to Tom... in this particular circumstance, Randy was certain he knew what Tom would do from his house two miles away.

He'd look at the alarm clock, see that he'd been robbed of sleep two hours before the alarm was due to go off, then curse a blue streak.

Then he'd be too upset to go back to sleep and would instead turn on his computer.

And log onto Facebook.

Randy stretched and turned on his own computer.

He logged onto Facebook himself, ignoring the friend requests from single women around Lubbock who'd stumbled across his profile and were impressed with his smile.

Or the fact that he was a Texas Ranger and they wanted to be a Ranger's girlfriend or wife.

He ignored the feed, where many of his friends had posted humorous memes or cell-phone photographs of whatever it was they had for dinner the previous evening.

He went directly to his chat list where a tiny green light told him that yes indeed, his good friend and partner Tom Cohen was on-line.

He picked up his cell phone and told his voice assistant to call Tom.

Tom picked it up on the second ring.

"Hey, Randy. What took you so long?"

It turned out that Tom could read Randy as well as Randy read Tom.

Not unlike an old married couple who'd been together for so long they could finish one another's sentences.

"Oh, I thought I'd let you doze a bit before I made you get up."

"Well, thanks for that."

"Anytime, my friend."

"Should I assume that you want to leave early, since we're up anyway?"

"You would assume correctly, my fine friend."

"How soon will you be ready?"

"Twenty minutes."

"See you in twenty five."

The nice thing about being out and about in Lubbock, Texas at two a.m. on a Tuesday morning was that the streets were almost deserted.

It was said that the only people on the streets in Lubbock at two a.m. were criminals and the policemen who were looking for them.

And two sleepy Texas Rangers on their way north of town to a tiny hamlet called Belton.

Chapter 27

The Rangers were Janice's first customers and enjoyed a nice relaxing breakfast, prepared by a short-order cook who knew his stuff.

Janice checked the parking lot for cars before she sat down beside Tom and asked how their "project" was coming.

It was obvious to Tom she was fishing for information, although it was impossible to tell whether it was merely curiosity or something else.

"We're still looking, but we're getting close to giving up. We're starting to think the tip we got was a red herring, that our bail jumpers are up in Nebraska. We're going to give it a couple more days and then head up that way"

"I'm sorry to hear that. I was hoping you'd catch them. You see, my daughter had some issues and I've got custody of my grandchildren. Two boys, ages six and ten. I don't like to leave them home alone while I'm at work, but this job don't pay enough for a babysitter. So they sit at home after school and watch TV and read, and play those damn video games. It's not a very exciting life for them, but I can't let them go outside while I'm gone. I just can't. The world has become too dangerous a place. Thank God my neighbor is there to get them on and off the school bus for me and to make sure the house is safe to go into every afternoon. I was hoping you guys would take a couple of bad dudes off the street and make it a little bit safer around here. And to be honest, I was hoping I could give you the tip you needed to find them, so I could get my car fixed."

She didn't appear to be asking for a handout, necessarily. But Randy got the sense she'd been hoping to be able to help them for her own benefit as well as their own.

As they'd driven past the diner a couple of days before they'd seen her in the parking lot, standing in front of an aging and beat-up Chevrolet, its hood up and steam coming from beneath it. She was pouring water from a gallon water jug into a hot radiator. The Rangers would have stopped to assist her, were it not for the tricked out Chevy Silverado pickup parked in an adjacent spot.

They could not jeopardize their operation by becoming visible to their targets, who might see them in the parking lot and start wondering who they were and why they were there.

So they'd passed her by, and Randy had felt guilty about it since.

"Maybe someday the streets will be safe enough for your kids to play outside again," Randy said as he rose to leave. "We'll let you know when we decide to leave town. By the way, I didn't catch your last name."

"Ramirez. Janice Ramirez."

Randy held out his hand to her and she took it, then left him to seat another customer.

The bill was only six dollars and change. For two breakfasts and two coffees, it was a pretty good deal.

Randy put it on his card and added a two dollar tip, on the upper side of average for a bill that size.

She wouldn't find the hundred dollar bill tucked up under Randy's plate until she went back a few minutes later to clear the table and wipe it down.

It wouldn't buy a new radiator. But it would help. And it would ease Randy's conscience. For although he understood it was a necessary part of his job, he hated to deceive people. He'd always been a straight shooter. It was just part of who he was.

Ninety minutes later Randy and Tom were back in their office, Tom at the computer and Randy looking over his shoulder.

"Jackpot!"

Randy couldn't hide the excitement in his voice as they watched high definition night vision footage of two men removing the tarp from the bed of the Silverado in the dead of night.

Beneath the tarp were compressed gas cylinders, cardboard boxes, and dozens of gallon jugs full of chemicals.

They watched as the men carried load after load into the bowels of the ranch house. At one point one of them tripped going up the steps of the darkened porch, the boxes he was carrying flying in all directions.

Tom couldn't help but laugh at the spectacle and lectured the men on the screen in front of him.

"If you guys would find an honest way to make a living, you'd be able to turn on your porch light without drawing attention to yourselves."

Randy said, "Well, it's obvious they're cooking meth. Do you think this is enough to get a search warrant?"

'I don't know. Let's show the major and see what he thinks."

Chapter 28

Major Shultz watched the video in dead silence, his left hand on the back of Tom's chair and his right hand rubbing his chin.

He waited until the very end, when the suspects finished unloading the truck and disappeared for good inside the ranch house, before providing his assessment.

"This in itself isn't much, in my opinion. I mean, just because we say those are materials for a meth lab doesn't necessarily make it so. You and I know it is, but any good defense attorney could cry foul.

"However, couple this with the fact that the vehicle belongs to a known drug kingpin, and I'd guess it's enough for a probable cause warrant. We'll take it before Judge Chancy. He's been in a hanging mood lately when it comes to drug manufacturers. I'm pretty sure he'll give us our warrant."

Judge John Chancy's nephew had been killed on the streets of Amarillo a few months before. He was walking down the street on his way to work at a local coffee house when a drug dealer mistook him for someone else.

Someone who'd ratted him out a year before and told the police he was cooking meth in an abandoned house on West Fifth Street.

The dealer, out on bond, emptied a ten round magazine into the helpless eighteen year old, then took the time to insert a second magazine and emptied it as well.

A police car on routine patrol two blocks away was attracted by the gunshots and came around the corner just in time for its dashboard camera to catch the killer firing the last three shots into the boy's body.

They had him dead to rights. And since Texas was a capital punishment state, he'd likely be put to death himself after the justice system did its usual song and dance.

That wouldn't bring back Judge Chancy's innocent nephew. Or raise the six week old baby he left behind.

But it was enough to sour the old judge's temperament when it came to things like the manufacture and distribution of illegal drugs.

Judges are supposed to be impartial and fair, and apply the letter and the spirit of the law in every decision they make.

But judges are human, too. They feel joy and pain like everyone else. They are capable of loving as easily as any other human being.

And they are just as capable of hate.

Judge Chancy hated drug people with a passion. While he had a bit of sympathy for the average street user, and realized many turned to drugs to escape the misery of a hopeless life, he gave no quarter and had no mercy for those higher on the food chain. The dealers, the manufacturers, the kingpins who took the least risk and reaped the greatest rewards.

If any judge in Texas would grant a probable cause warrant based on the scant evidence the Rangers had, it was Judge John Chancy.

In the end, it wasn't even in question. With a stroke of the old judge's pen, the Rangers had a legal right to swoop in on the ranch house and search it, then to seize everything in it having anything to do with the manufacture and distribution of illegal drugs.

And to arrest anyone on the premises, whether they had an outstanding warrant or not.

Late in the afternoon Tom and Randy met once again in Major Shultz's office to discuss their takedown plan.

Joining them were two agents from the Federal Bureau of Investigation, Agent Choate and Agent Gonzalez. Agent Gonzalez was fluent in Spanish, which could well come in handy in such an operation.

"The owner of the property resides in New Mexico," the major began. "That makes this a multi-state operation and makes it a federal case. That's good because the FBI's got more manpower than we do. We can't count on the local cops to help, since we don't know which of them besides the chief might be caught up in it. We'll go in early in the morning, when there's likely to be only one patrol car on shift. We'll find him with one of the fed's unmarked cars and will keep him off his radio and occupied until after the takedown is finished. Then we'll hit the police station and secure it before they know what hit them. Just in case Chief Bennett has any evidence we can use in his office."

Randy asked an obvious question.

"Do we have enough for an arrest warrant for the chief?"

"Yes. We have a sworn affidavit from two confidential informants that place him at the ranch house at least twice in the past few weeks. The meet with the Silverado you guys got on tape is just icing on the cake. We'll have a separate takedown crew who will roust him out of bed at the same time we hit the ranch house. And we'll scramble the cell phone signals at the ranch house so they can't give him any advance warning. We don't want him flushing anything down his toilet while we're getting ready to knock down his front door."

Tom asked, "Where will Randy and I be?"

"You'll be on the team at the ranch house. The FBI and federal marshals will take the chief into custody, and will put the patrolman on ice until we can determine who else needs to be questioned."

The prearranged "go" time was 4:30 a.m. It was widely regarded as the best possible time to spring such an invasion of a drug laboratory, for several reasons.

Most labs didn't run twenty four operations. They shut down at night and rested, like most other businesses both legal and otherwise.

And most lab workers lived on the premises. So it was logical to assume that at 4:30 a.m. most of them would be in bed sleeping.

It was also a good time to catch sentries dozing off, since they'd be nearing the end of their shifts.

Lastly, at 4:30 a.m. it was still dark enough to cover the takedown team's movements as they crept toward the ranch house in black vehicles with no lights, or on foot in black clothing.

And 4:30 a.m. was the most peaceful time of the day, when the last thing anyone would expect would be twenty heavily armed men getting into position to swarm in and take control.

The group finalized the plans, assigned duties, and made preparations to go.

Chapter 29

At three thirty four black panel vans drove north on Highway 87 and passed the ranch house on the east side of the highway. There was no moon on this particular night, and it was partly cloudy. The vans were practically invisible when they blacked out their lights a half mile farther up the highway and pulled onto an unmarked and unnamed dirt road.

The road was normally used by a cotton farmer to park his tractor and implements on when he wasn't using them. It was on private land and the farmer's cotton crop had already been stripped. The harvest was done for the year. There was no chance, none whatsoever, of anyone needing to use this particular road on this particular day.

From the vans emerged twenty men, dressed in black, half of them equipped with night vision goggles.

The ones so equipped disappeared silently into the night, moving across the farmer's field toward the ranch house. No more talk was needed. They had their marching orders and knew where to go. They would take up positions on all four corners of the house, in teams of three. They were the perimeter team, and it was their job to take down any bad guys who tried to escape once the warrant team made their presence known at the front of the house.

The perimeter team needed a few extra minutes to get into position, so the warrant team went over the process between themselves while they waited.

The leader, Agent Sorenson, called over his shoulder microphone to his field team.

"Able Seven, have you found him yet?"

"Roger. Closing in on him now."

Able Seven consisted of two agents in an unmarked Crown Victoria. It was one of those cars that law enforcement officers drive to be inconspicuous, but which everyone can spot from a mile away. Black tires, no hubcaps, dull color, no chrome. At least this one didn't have a tell-tale spotlight mounted over the driver's side mirror.

Able Seven already knew there was only one patrolman on the streets in Belton on any given weeknight. It was just a matter of cruising up and down the streets of the tiny town until they stumbled across him.

And it didn't take them long. Just as Agent Sorenson called them, asking for their status, they spotted the patrol car parked in front of the town's only 7-Eleven.

They pulled into the parking lot, parked at a gas pump, and walked into the store.

Officer Cody Lester was a pudgy man in his early thirties who wouldn't have been on solo patrol in most cities. He wouldn't have been able to chase down a suspect without having to stop for air every hundred yards. And he'd have been so slow he wouldn't have had a chance of catching them anyway. In all likelihood, if he'd been assigned to a "real department," he'd have been on the fat-boy program, forced to lose so many pounds a week or face suspension. Forced to spend some of his off-duty hours at the local gym to get back into shape.

When the two FBI agents found him, he was a walking talking billboard reflecting every stereotypical concept of the American policeman. He had a cup of coffee in one hand, a donut in the other, and was trying to make time with the middle-aged night clerk.

The agents walked in and didn't even earn a glance from Officer Lester.

Any policeman, especially those on duty in the dead of night, should be aware of their surroundings. They're trained to look at everyone, and to assess them immediately. To determine whether they're acting suspiciously. Whether they should be where they're at and doing what they're doing. It's a key part of a patrolman's job.

But Officer Lester couldn't be bothered. He was too busy trying to impress the night clerk out of her oversized pants.

The agents walked up behind him, their IDs out in front of them.

"Good evening, officer. Can we talk to you for a minute?"

Lester looked up, not happy to be interrupted.

His face changed instantly from one of annoyance to one of fear when he saw the two men.

He knew they were feds even without seeing their credentials. Federal officers have a certain look about them. Even when they were wearing blue jeans and button down sports shirts instead of the traditional black suits.

The 9mm handguns attached to their belts was another not-so-subtle clue.

Lester stood bolt upright, almost at the position of attention, and sucked in his gut.

He didn't even realize he dropped his half-eaten donut on the sales counter.

"Y-y-yes, sir."

"Agent Mike Donnelly. FBI. This is Agent Spang."

"Yes, sir."

Agent Donnelly produced a folded piece of paper from his back pocket.

"I have an order from a federal court judge to detain you and to ask you some questions. Do you want to read it?"

"Um…"

Lester's face was flushed. His knees were weak and he suddenly felt nauseated. He wished he were somewhere else. *Anywhere* else.

Donnelly didn't have all morning to wait for an answer. He slapped the paper on the counter in front of a frightened Officer Lester. When Donnelly stepped away from the counter again, he was disgusted to step in a puddle of liquid next to Lester's right shoe.

It was urine. Lester didn't even notice he was peeing his pants, until Donnelly looked down at the floor and then into Lester's face.

"Do not use your radio, even if your dispatcher or chief calls you. Do you understand?"

"Yes, sir. I won't, I swear."

Then it finally dawned on the young officer. He suddenly knew why the feds had gotten the drop on him.

"This is about Chief Bennett and his dealings with those drug people, isn't it?"

Donnelly smiled. It wasn't supposed to be this easy. But he wasn't about to question a gift from the gods.

"Hold that thought, officer. We'll get back to it in just a minute."

Donnelly keyed his microphone and sent a brief transmission over the airways.

"This is Able Seven. Subject is being detained."

Chapter 30

Once the only patrol officer in Belton was neutralized, there was little chance of Chief Bennett finding out about the takedown until it was too late.

When all four corners of the ranch house were covered, the warrant team climbed back into the panel vans and crept silently into the front yard of the ranch house. When they were about halfway there Perimeter Team Two called into the command center to report they'd cut water from the well house to the house.

If anyone in the house tried to flush any evidence, they'd have to be thorough. They'd only have one flush to do it. Then there would be no more water in the toilet's tank.

The warrant team dispersed around the building, taking up positions at both doors. All had their service weapons charged and at the ready position while they waited for all hell to break loose.

As the officers who secured the evidence needed for the takedown, Randy and Tom would be given the prestigious honor of serving the warrant. They and two federal agents rapped loudly on the frame of the door with a nightstick.

Two other FBI agents stood by with a battering ram in case the door didn't open quickly enough to suit them.

Randy yelled out in a loud and clear voice.

"State and federal agents with a search warrant. You have twenty seconds to open this door, or we're coming in."

Special Agent Gonzalez repeated the orders in Spanish.

Randy, his back flat against the wall beside the door, had his head turned toward a large picture window overlooking the front porch. He saw the curtain move and heard shouting on the inside of the house. In Spanish.

The seconds ticked by.

The battering ram team stepped onto the porch and stood at the ready, and were taking their first backswing when the door suddenly opened.

An old woman opened the door and stepped aside, allowing the officers in. Officers at the back door came bursting in, weapons drawn, ready and willing to shoot anyone who appeared to threaten them in the slightest way.

But there was no resistance. In the end, the bad guys all went peacefully. There was no gunfire, no arguments. In the end there were only tears. Lots and lots of tears.

And denials. To a man, every person in the ranch house, including the old woman, claimed they were merely ranch workers who fed horses and cattle and kept the place clean.

It was not an uncommon tactic. Everyone had been told ahead of time that if they were ever busted, to pretend to be an innocent merely caught up in circumstance. Let the gringos sort everyone out, it was said, and try to find evidence on each individual which would link him or her to the lab. Odds were they couldn't. At least for the majority of the workers.

And that was the way it once worked. In the past, many such worker bees at a drug manufacturing lab were set free. Simply because it couldn't be proven that they were more than what they claimed to be: a maid, a ranch hand, a cook.

But then the new tactic came along to prosecute people for organized crime, regardless of what role they had to play in the process. And under the new rules, even cooks, maids and ranch hands could be charged as accessories.

Now it was possible to charge all of them, regardless of what minor role they may have played in the operation. And certainly, some innocents probably did get sent away for long periods of time.

But more often than not the people claiming minor roles were in the muck a lot deeper than they'd claimed. And under the new process they could be sent away for long prison terms even if there was no direct evidence against them.

By five a.m. little Belton, Texas had become a little more like it used to be. A peaceful little town. Sleepy by most standards. And relatively crime free.

The largest crystal methamphetamine lab in the history of North Texas was now officially on ice.

No pun intended.

Chapter 31

Fallout from the Belton bust touched every corner of Texas and far beyond.

Belton Police Chief Ron Bennett saw the other side of his jail's bars for the first time. It was only temporary, until the feds could transfer him to Dallas to face federal charges.

But it was long enough to make him cry like a baby and beg the federal officers for forgiveness.

For disgracing his badge and oath of office.

Actually, he felt no guilt at all. He just thought he could curry favor with the FBI by professing his regret, in hopes they'd somehow set him free and go after the bigger fish instead.

Fat chance.

It was a dreadful miscalculation on Chief Bennett's part, which he didn't realize until his attorney showed up at his jail cell to consult with him.

The lawyer asked Agent Donnelly, "Did you Mirandize him?"

"Yes, sir. Got it on video."

Then counsel turned back to Bennett and said, "Shut up, you old fool. I'm afraid you've just *regretted* your way into a twenty year sentence."

Bennett sobbed even louder and said, "No. It can't be. I was supposed to retire next year."

And that had been his plan. To retire and to take the "cash out" option of the modest pension the city of Belton had planned to give him. And to use that money to buy a small recreational vehicle. He and the wife would spend the rest of their natural lives, touring the country and bouncing from one grandchild's house to another. All the while, they would pay for everything they needed along the way with hundred dollar bills.

Hundred dollar bills from the stash of half a million dollars they'd squirreled away in the two previous years.

Money he'd earned by running interference for the biggest drug cartel in all of Mexico, and making sure their Belton manufacturing operation never saw any heat from the law.

Now Bennett would never see his RV. Never travel the states near and far.

Indeed, never see his wife again. For she dropped dead of a heart attack upon hearing the news that her husband had been arrested and would probably spend the rest of his life behind prison walls.

Several of the supposed cooks, maids and ranch hands saw the writing on the wall and knew they were in for long prison terms themselves.

Some were okay with it. In some circles prison time is viewed as a badge of honor.

But others decided it wasn't what they signed up for. Others decided it was better to snitch. To name names in exchange for lighter sentences. Or for deportation back to Mexico, where they'd spend the rest of their lives running from the cartel. The cartels didn't like snitches at all.

Over the course of a few weeks, arrest warrants would be issued against more than two dozen drug kingpins. A few were known to be in the United States, but most were in Mexico. And so began the long and painful process of extraditing the kingpins for trial.

Few would ever set foot on American soil. The Mexican judicial system was too corrupt for anyone with any pull or money to be extradited. Only those the Mexican judges had vendettas against, or those whose judges were in the pockets of rival cartels would be sent back for trial.

If, of course, their own cartels didn't take them out before their extradition to keep them from becoming snitches as well.

Truth be known, the Belton bust wouldn't shut down any of the Mexican drug trade. It stung, in the same way a bee sting might cause one to curse and swear bloody revenge against the tiny creatures.

But the Belton operation was merely a single cog in a giant machine. Its takedown was but a small burp to the process. Nothing more.

The Belton bust would, unfortunately, do no permanent damage to the Mexican drug trade.

The junkies, on the other hand, felt the pain.

The price of a gram of crystal meth in northern and west Texas jumped from seventy dollars to three hundred overnight. And the ice that was available was cut so much it was almost worthless.

It was quite literally more artificial sweetener and crushed rock salt than dope.

On the face of it, that should have brought smiles to the faces of those in law enforcement whose job it was to eliminate illegal drugs from the streets of Lubbock, Amarillo, and a dozen other towns.

Chapter 32

And it did help. A little.

Word got out that crystal meth was now very hard to come by. That the higher price was appropriate, because traffickers had to drive it in from Denver, or set up small labs themselves and cook their own.

Word also got around that it would be that way for at least several months, until the cartels managed to set up another lab similar to the one at Belton and get it up and running.

Nobody wanted to wait that long. And nobody wanted to pay three hundred dollars for a gram of dope that had very little dope in it.

Some of the more mobile junkies simply left Texas and went elsewhere. Texas law officers were happy about that, but they weren't welcomed in Oklahoma City, or Albuquerque or Denver, or wherever they wound up.

The bust drove some of the hardcore junkies in to seek medical treatment. To finally throw in the towel and admit they had a problem and to try to get off the ice. Some of them would succeed. Some would find abstinence more painful than they'd realized, and would wash out of the program.

Casual users, the one with no monkey on their backs, simply walked away from it. Or turned to something that was easier to get. Marijuana prices in Lubbock and Amarillo went up as demand increased.

Crime in the two cities most impacted by the Belton bust decreased, but not as much as it was hoped. Property crime like burglaries pretty much stayed the same. There were fewer meth users who needed to steal from day to day to feed their habits, sure.

But those who remained had to pay a lot more for their dope, and therefore had to steal more than they'd stolen in the past.

In the end it was a victory for law enforcement and a minor setback for the cartels. Chief Bennett spent three days in lockup, protected from two other inmates who understandably didn't think much of the man who'd put them behind bars. After he made bail he no-showed his wife's funeral, choosing instead to stay at home. Sitting on his favorite recliner with his feet propped up, he pulled out a .38 revolver and shot himself in the head.

He didn't leave a note explaining why, or to apologize to his children for leaving a big mess for them to clean up.

But everyone knew why he did it.

Some of the hardest time in the Texas penitentiary system is as a cop gone bad. They are targeted by other inmates and are usually segregated from the rest of the prison population for twenty three hours of each and every day. Their food is spat in or tainted with all manner of other disgusting things.

Those who tire of being in solitary confinement are allowed to request reassignment to general population, but they do so at their own risk. They exchange the loneliness of a single-man cell for having to watch their backs twenty four-seven. It's a given that at some point, sometimes toward the end of their prison term, they'll be stabbed in the back with a homemade shank or beaten to unconsciousness by a prison gang who dislikes cops.

One of the bright spots in the Belton takedown was the day Randy and Tom paid a visit to the tiny diner on Highway 87 and asked for Janice.

"Remember us?"

"Sure. You're those two bounty hunters who turned out to be Texas Rangers instead."

"Are you mad at us for deceiving you?"

"Are you kidding? I never told you that my oldest grandson had been hanging around with a bunch of meth users. It was only a matter of time before he tried it. Now it's damn near impossible to get in Belton, and he doesn't have a car to drive to Amarillo or Lubbock to get it. So now I can sleep just a little bit easier. All I have to worry about is him getting involved in a gang or shoplifting or getting his girlfriend pregnant or dropping out of high school. The usual things that keep a single parent up at night. But at least now there's one less thing on that list, so thank you guys for that."

"How's the car running these days?"

"It's in the shop. Again. I finally saved enough tips to get the radiator replaced. Now the transmission is out. I hate cars. Sometimes I wish we'd go back to the days of riding horses. If your horse broke down all you had to do was shoot it and steal somebody else's."

Tom got a sour look on his face and she laughed.

"Just kidding, fellas. I wouldn't want you guys coming after me. Hey, are you here for breakfast? Sit in one of the booths and I'll bring you some menus."

Randy said, "No. Actually, ma'am, we just stopped off to give you something."

She didn't skip a beat.

"If it's an engagement ring, I'll pass. I've been married twice, and how I managed to find the two biggest losers in the state of Texas is beyond me. But I've given up on marriage. So as handsome and charming as you two guys are, I'll have to pass. Sorry."

Randy countered, "No rings today. But this may help fix your transportation problem."

He held out a check in front of him. A check for thirty thousand dollars, made out to Janice Ramirez.

Tom reached out and grabbed her arm to steady her. She looked ready to pass out.

And she lost her voice for a few seconds.

Finally, she managed a few words.

"Why? And how?"

"You've probably never heard of the seizure and reward fund. Most people haven't. The Texas legislature decreed a few years back that all property seized in drug busts like the one here in Belton became the property of the State of Texas. The ranch house, the money in it, all vehicles attached to the operation. It's a way of making the drug cartels help pay for their own demise.

"As part of the legislation, up to ten percent of the cash seized goes into a fund to reward good citizens who helped bring the operation to light. There are several others who provided tips as to what was going on, and we submitted your name as well. We hope you don't mind."

Janice didn't know what to say.

"But… but…"

Then she found two words that said it all.

"Thank you."

"You don't have to thank us. You pointed out our suspects and the vehicle they drove. You didn't know you were helping out the Texas Rangers on a police corruption case, but it still counts."

She got teary-eyed.

"I honestly don't know what to say. Would you sit down and have some breakfast? It's on me this time. And I'll make sure it's the best breakfast you've ever had, even if I have to go back there and shove Lenny away from the grill and make it myself."

Randy looked at Tom and asked, "Are you in any big hurry to get back to Lubbock and ask the major for our next assignment?"

"I'm never in any hurry to see the major, no matter what we're asking him."

Randy turned back to Janice and said, "Count us in."

Chapter 33

Randy knocked on the wall next to their commanding officer's door.

Major Shultz looked up from a stack of papers he was reading and said, "Come in, you two."

"Good morning, sir. We just wanted to give you an update on the Belton case."

"Good. Sit down, men. Bring me up to speed."

"Most of the local suspects have bonded out of jail. The Mexican nationals among them are being held without bail, as is one Jesse Ortiz, who it turns out is wanted for a triple murder in northern California."

Shultz raised his eyebrows.

"Oh?"

"Yes. The FBI says they think he's an enforcer for the cartel. The three victims in California were manufacturers in one of their meth labs who turned state's evidence and were targeted as snitches. The feds think it's a new tactic for the cartel. To place an enforcer in their midst to take out anyone who gets disgruntled or sloppy, or who hints he might snitch at some point."

"Well, that's a troubling turn of events. But it didn't seem to work in this case, did it?"

"Apparently not. They apparently didn't make him. Several of them are competing with the district attorney to cut deals. They're naming big names."

"Yeah. Too bad all the really big names are south of the border and untouchable. But we'll get a lot of the medium sized fish and slow them down a bit."

"Yes sir."

"Any loose ends that need to be tied up?"

"No sir. The state's attorney said they'll let us know about trial dates a few weeks out so we can plan for them. We handed out reward checks to four confidential informants this morning and made some people very happy. As of now, we're considering this one closed and ready for a new assignment."

"I'll tell you what, boys. I don't like either one of you. You know that. There's just something about you that makes my skin crawl. But I'd be one heartless commander indeed if I gave you a new case on a Friday morning. How about you take the rest of the day off and go fishing or something? I'll have a new case on your desks first thing Monday morning."

Randy looked at Tom and shrugged his shoulders. Tom said, "Sounds good to us, and thanks, boss. See you Monday."

They made it almost to the door when Shultz stopped them.

"Hey Tom?"

"Yes sir?"

"How's that riding project coming?"

Tom rolled his eyes.

"Just fine, sir. I'm practically ready for the next rodeo."

Shultz turned to Randy.

"Is that true?"

Randy hesitated.

"Well? As his riding instructor it's your responsibility to give me an honest assessment."

"Well, sir…. Let's just say he hasn't fallen off his horse for the last two lessons. So that's a big improvement for him."

Tom winced.

The major smiled.

"That's good. Real good. I signed you both up for the Northern Division's mounted regiment. You'll be riding in the city's Fourth of July parade down Broadway each year. All decked out in your dress uniforms, looking as spiffy as you can be."

He turned his head and eyed Tom.

"Don't embarrass the Rangers by falling off your horse during the parade, Tom. Or next year you'll be on foot, following the horses with a big pooper scooper."

"Yes, sir."

Randy chuckled.

"Maybe instead of taking the rest of the day off we should hit the stables."

Tom said, "Peachy. Just peachy."

Chapter 34

The Rangers had lunch at a local barbeque grill and then rode until the sun started to dip into the western sky.

"I've traveled all over the world," Tom told his friend. "I was a military brat. My dad was in the Air Force. I lived in Europe and in Korea and in five different states before he retired here in Texas. In all the places I've been in my life I've never seen any sunsets as pretty as the ones in Texas."

"No doubt. Let's get the gear put away and brush them down."

"That won't take but an hour or so. The night's still young. You want to go clubbing? I know you don't drink, but I do. Maybe we can meet a couple of girls and get lucky."

Randy rolled his eyes. It was an old story. His friends were always inviting him to go along so he could be their designated driver. That enabled them to get sloshed and not have to worry about making it home safely. They knew that Randy had their backs.

He didn't mind, necessarily. He enjoyed cutting back and having a drink or two sometimes too. Even if his drink of choice was Dr. Pepper with peanuts.

"I would, Tom. But I told the major I'd spend a night in the office this weekend. So I can tell him once and for all whether the ghost of Henry Jenkins really haunts the place. I was going to run by my apartment and get a good book to read and then hang out there tonight."

"I'll tell you what, Randy. I've been kind of curious about the whole ghost story nonsense myself. I'll make a deal with you. No self-respecting ghost comes out until midnight. Everybody knows that. Let's hit a couple of bars and then cut out at eleven. That'll give us time to gear up and make it to the office by midnight."

"So you're going to spend the night there too?"

"Sure. Wouldn't want you to go up against that big bad spooky ghost yourself. We're partners, after all. If you have my back at the clubs, I'll have your back at the office. Fair enough?"

Randy thought for a minute.

He wasn't afraid of any ghosts he expected to encounter during the night. But being alone in the office for the whole night would get a bit boring without someone else to talk to. It would be a lot easier to stay awake all night with someone to keep him company.

"Okay. Deal. But what did you mean, gear up?"

"You know. You get your book, and I get my video games."

"Oh. Of course."

The two parted ways and made plans for Randy to pick Tom up around eight p.m.

Randy's role was to enjoy the company of his friends and play chauffeur. He had no qualms about it, but his role left no say so regarding where they went or how long they'd stay there. He'd leave that up to Tom.

They started out at a local diner called the Mean Woman Grill. Randy was a bit leery at first, given the name. But Tom was quick to reassure him.

"Best food in ten counties, bar none," he said. "Try their chicken fried steak. It's hand chopped, hand breaded, and fried in a skillet. Just like your mama used to make. It doesn't come out of a white box, pre-cooked and frozen, like other places do it. Try it. If you don't like it, it's on me."

"It's on you anyway, Tom. I bought lunch, remember?"

"Oh, yeah. Anyway, if it seems the building is shaped funny it's because it used to be a 7-Eleven. I lived over there on 6th Street when I was little and my dad was stationed at the base here. I used to walk here to spend my pennies and nickels on candy bars. Anyway, they closed it down for awhile, and then these folks bought it, knocked out the west wall and expanded it, and made a restaurant out of it. Like I said, best food in twenty counties."

"You said ten counties a minute ago."

"Yeah, well, their reputation is growing even as we speak."

But Randy didn't hear him. Randy was watching one of the prettiest women he'd seen since he came to Lubbock. She was on a small stage in the corner of the restaurant, strumming on an electric acoustic guitar and singing a love song.

"Tom, who is *that*?"

"That's Jenni Dale Lord. She plays here a couple of times a month. She's the other best reason to come here."

"She's gorgeous. And she sings... she's just amazing."

"Right on both accounts, my friend. It's okay to be smitten by her. Everybody falls for her. But don't you try to go marry her or anything. She's gonna marry me. She just doesn't know it yet."

"Marry you? Have you asked her?"

"Oh, yeah. At least twenty times. She keeps telling me no. But I'll wear her down, you wait and see. Someday she's gonna be playing on tour in all the big venues, all over the world. And I'll be along as her husband and unofficial tour manager and t-shirt counter."

"Sounds like you've got it bad for her."

"Well, like I said, a lot of us do. But she'll marry me someday, you'll see."

"Can I help you?"

Randy looked up to see a pretty young waitress, order book in hand.

"Hi. My friend here says I have to try your chicken fried steak. Medium rare, extra gravy. With all the trimmings."

"And to drink?"

"Dr. Pepper, in the bottle. With peanuts if you have any."

She didn't bat an eye. Must be a local girl, he suspected.

"And for you, sir?"

"Your green chili cheeseburger, side of Fritos. And a Bud Light, no peanuts."

She smiled and said, "Coming right up," then disappeared.

Randy said, "Wait a minute. You went on and on about the chicken fried steak. And then you didn't even get it. How come?"

"Because I couldn't decide between it and my second favorite thing on the menu, the green chili cheeseburger. This way I can have the burger, and still have whatever steak you have left on your plate."

"What if there isn't any?"

"There will be. I've seen you eat. You eat like a teenage girl on a diet."

Chapter 35

Tom was right about a lot of things that night. The chicken fried steak was, as he'd predicted, the best that Randy had ever eaten.

He did indeed, as he promised, propose to the young singer during one of her breaks.

And she did indeed tell him no, although she did it with a sweet smile that kept his heart from being broken. He told her he'd ask her again and she told him to go ahead. It had become a tradition between two good friends.

Randy made a mental note to come back to the Mean Woman Grill every chance he got. Or at least until he tried every item on the menu. This after hearing other customers argue out loud about which was the best dish the kitchen served.

Their next stop was a tiny bar across the street from Lubbock's famous Cactus Theater.

The pair seemed oddly out of place, being the only two men in the joint with cowboy hats. But the staff was friendly and the rock and roll music being spun was good. They decided to stay and wait for a couple of other Rangers to finish their shift and join them.

They sat at a table for four, and the two empty chairs were too tempting for a couple of girls to resist.

One was tall and stunning, with thick chestnut hair stretching to the small of her back. The other was shorter, a blonde, with cute freckles scattered about a cherubic face. She was, as Randy's grandpa would have said, cuter than a June bug's ear.

Randy had heard him say that a thousand times, and still wasn't sure what it meant.

The blonde pulled one of the chairs out and plopped herself into it.

Or maybe poured would be a better description.

She put two tequila shots on the table in front of her, miraculously managing not to spill either one.

She slurred, "Mine if we sid down?"

Randy smiled his good-old-boy smile.

"Not at all. Please sit down."

"Shank you very much. I kinda already did."

"Yes indeed you did."

"I wanna tell you someshin, cowboy."

She suddenly turned to her friend and giggled.

"Did ya hear dat, Sarah? I called him a cowboy."

"Yes, sweetie. I heard it."

The brunette looked apologetically at Randy, then Tom.

The Rangers didn't mind. They were amused and enjoying the show.

Randy asked the drunk one, "What did you want to tell me, honey?"

"Oh, did ya hear that, Sarah? He called me honey."

Sarah rolled her eyes.

"I heard him, Rachel."

"Wait, wait, wait, damn it. I gots someshin I wanna say."

"Go ahead, honey."

"I just wanna shay that... I don' 'member."

She looked at Sarah and asked for help.

"What was I gonna shay again?"

Then the light came on in her eyes.

"Oh, yeah. I jus' wanna shay, cowboy, that I lubs you."

With that, she placed her forehead gently on the table between the two shot glasses and passed out.

Tom looked at Randy and said, "She loves you, partner."

"So I heard."

Both men watched her for several seconds to see if there would be any more. But she was out like a light.

Randy turned his attention instead to her friend.

"I'm Randy. This here is my friend Tom."

The brunette, who appeared to be stone sober, reached out and shook both their hands.

"I feel I should have to apologize for my friend. I'm so sorry."

"Think nothing of it," Randy said while giving Tom a sideways glance. "I have to apologize for my friend all the time too. What was that all about, exactly?"

"Well, she brings me along as her designated driver, every time she breaks up with a boyfriend. That way she can get wasted while she's hunting for the next one."

Randy smiled.

"And I assume I somehow made it into her sights."

"Exactly. See, we've never been into this particular bar before. They play rock and roll, and it's good stuff, but usually we go to country bars."

As though she felt a need to prove her point, she lifted one leg high enough for Randy and Tom to see she was wearing cowboy boots.

"Anyway, we felt a little bit out of place, until we saw you guys walk in. And the first thing she said to me was, 'Look at that tall one. I'm going to take him home tonight.'"

Tom interjected, "It seems to me that you're not much of a friend."

The girl sat back in her chair and said, "Excuse me?"

Tom continued, "Well, what I mean is, if you were a true friend, you'd have pointed out that I'm the much better looking of us two. Randy looks like he just waded three miles through Swamp Ugly. And he has no personality either. If you were a true friend you'd have pointed out how handsome I was and suggested she take me home instead of him."

She laughed and said, "Oh, is that so?"

Randy said, "We know your name is Sarah. Do you have a last name to go with it?"

"Sarah Anna Speer."

"I'm Randy Maloney. The handsome one with the personality is Tom Cohen. He's actually a wolf in sheep's clothing. But you'll find that out soon enough."

"No doubt. So, are you guys working at one of the ranches around here?"

"No. Actually we're Texas Rangers."

"No you're not."

Randy looked at Tom, who shrugged.

"She says we're not."

"Well, the lady couldn't possibly be wrong. She's much too pretty to be wrong. So I guess we're not."

"Well, what are we, then?"

"You just escaped from a mental hospital and I was sent to track you down."

"Then why are we here, sitting at a bar with two pretty girls?"

"Because I've got a big heart. And I'm not going to take you back to the asylum without letting you enjoy at least one beer. And I wanted a Dr. Pepper with peanuts. It was a win-win decision."

Sarah said, "Okay. That's enough, you two. Are you really Texas Rangers?"

Randy tipped his Stetson.

"Yes, ma'am. We really are."

"I still don't believe you. Show me your badges."

Chapter 36

"Well I'll be darned," she said while examining the two badges side by side. "I thought Texas Rangers only existed on that TV show and in Austin."

"Well, the TV show is about as realistic as Santa's elves. And our headquarters is in Austin, but there's a handful of us stationed here in Lubbock."

"Where's your office?"

Across Broadway from the courthouse. In the federal building.

"And why are you here? In Lubbock, I mean."

"We go around to bars so drunk women can profess their love to us and then pass out."

"*Profess*? You're the first cowboy I've heard who uses that particular word. Are you smart or something?"

"Well, my mom used to say I was smarter than the average bear. But she might have just been trying to build up my self-esteem."

"How come your badge is beat all to hell, and his is shiny and new?"

"He has what they call a junior badge. It's like a trainer badge. They won't give him a real one until he knows how to tie his shoes and recite the alphabet properly two out of three times."

"No. Seriously."

"I come from a long line of Texas Rangers. That's the badge my great great grandfather wore. It's been passed down the line to each generation and finally to me. I'll be the last one to wear it, though."

"Wow, that's way cool. But how come you'll be the last one to wear it?"

"I've decided to retire the family tradition. And to return the badge to my great great grandfather, where it belongs."

"He's still alive? He must be, like a zillion years old."

"No. He passed away in 1931. I plan to bury the badge next to his headstone."

"So, how come you don't want your sons to carry on the tradition?"

"I just think it's time to get out of the law enforcement game. Into something safer. I used to watch my mom cry herself to sleep at night, worrying about my father. Being the wife of a lawman is tough. Very tough. And when I marry I don't want to put my wife through that. I don't want my kids to either."

"So, you're not married?"

"No."

"That's nice to know. I mean, a lot of these guys in here are. But their wives are conspicuously missing. So are their wedding bands. So it's always good to ask."

Tom, eager to be involved in the conversation, offered his two cents.

"Hey, I'm not married either. Single as can be. That's me, yes siree."

They ignored him.

Randy asked, "So… what do you do? I mean, when you're not escorting your inebriated friend and letting her fall asleep and drool all over the table?"

Sarah smiled and looked at Rachel, who had deposited an impressive amount of saliva into a puddle beneath her face.

"Should I take her photo, so I can put it on Facebook in the morning?"

"I'd say you probably shouldn't. I think she'll be embarrassed enough as it is."

"You don't know Rachel. She knows no shame."

"So, what *do* you do?"

"I'm a personal trainer at a gym on 34th Street."

Tom saw an opportunity to be relevant.

"Hey, I've been looking for a personal trainer. You need another client?"

But it was too late. Sarah was enamored by Randy's good looks and charm. Tom might as well have been on another planet.

She turned her head toward him and asked, "I'm sorry. Did you say something?"

"Never mind."

She went back to Randy.

"You know, my daddy used to put peanuts in his Dr. Pepper too."

"Then he must have been down home, like my family."

"I reckon so, cowboy. Hey, can you help me get Rachel to the car so I can take her home?"

"Sure."

Tom started looking around the bar to see if there were any other girls he could flirt with. This one was obviously smitten.

Randy picked Rachel up from her chair and carried her outside, Sarah clearing a path between the other patrons and tables.

He returned ten minutes later, a small piece of paper in hand with Sarah's phone number on it.

Tom asked, "I suppose you're going to keep that to yourself?"

"Yep."

"Figures."

Chapter 37

The other Rangers failed to show up, having had to work much longer than they'd planned. It was the life of a Ranger. Planning was frowned upon, because plans were too frequently broken. But the mission had to come first. The Rangers had a reputation and lineage few other agencies could match. And they didn't want sloppy work or lackadaisical attitudes to tarnish that reputation.

As promised, Tom was ready to go at eleven p.m.

Randy dropped his friend off and went home to get a book and make a couple of sandwiches. It would be a long night indeed without something to fill his stomach.

Then he went back and made two more sandwiches for Tom.

Tom was known to be a mooch. Every time they worked together on a long stakeout, Tom failed to bring his own food and wound up begging Randy for some of his.

And tonight's mission, after all, was a stake-out of sorts. By first light the next morning, Randy hoped to either prove the existence of Henry Jenkins' ghost, or to disprove it and put the matter to rest once and for all.

He loaded his things into the bed of his pickup and drove back to Tom's house, pulling into Tom's driveway and tapping his horn briefly.

It was too bad Randy was swigging his Dr. Pepper when Randy came out of his house. Randy was caught mid-swallow when the spectacle of Tom and his outfit caused him to gasp, then cough, then spray Dr. Pepper through his nostrils.

Then wince. For ice cold Dr. Pepper burns when one sprays it through their nostrils.

Tom emerged from his house, his bulletproof vest donned over a white t-shirt, wearing a Star Wars Stormtrooper helmet and sporting a light saber. He carried a galvanized trash can lid as a shield and had a white towel tied around his neck as a superhero cape.

Randy hadn't done such a thing since he was four.

Randy couldn't help but laugh out loud at the ridiculous sight, even as he was wiping Dr. Pepper off his chest and trying to catch his breath.

Tom climbed into the cab and said, "Let's go, partner. That ghost don't scare me."

Chapter 38

The third floor of the Mahon Federal Building was deserted, save for a lonely janitor mopping some dried vomit from the west end of the hallway.

He didn't bat an eye when Tom walked off the elevator, still wearing his ridiculous outfit. Randy, not wanting to be seen with his partner, took the stairs and arrived at the same time.

Randy said, "Go on without me. Start some coffee and I'll be there in a minute."

"You want me to go in there alone?"

"Don't worry. You have your light saber to protect you."

Randy walked to the end of the hallway and asked, "Hey, partner. My name's Randy. What's yours?"

The old man stopped mopping and leaned on his mop. Randy noticed for the first time how aged he was. For a second he thought about asking him if he knew a cowboy named Henry Jenkins personally.

But that would make the janitor a hundred and fifty years old. And he didn't look a day over a hundred and forty.

"Say, I'm a Ranger assigned to the office at the other end of the hall. I was just wondering if you've ever heard any strange noises coming from the part of the building."

"We don't clean your offices, son. Each agency has the option of providing their own cleaning. The Rangers have a custodial service that comes during the daytime to empty your trash and tidy up."

Come to think of it, Randy had indeed seen a young Hispanic woman come through the offices during the day to collect his garbage and sweep the floors.

The old man went on.

"The maintenance I do stops at the outer door. What kind of noises are you talking about?"

"I'm not sure, sir. Anything that sounds out of place, I guess. I just heard a rumor there might be a ghost in there."

The old man chuckled.

"Aren't you a little old to be believing in ghosts, young fella?"

"Yeah, probably. Thank you for your time."

Randy turned and started walking toward his office. The janitor noticed a spot on the floor he'd missed and went back over it a second time.

Randy was almost to his office door when the man called out, "You mean the sick guy?"

He turned around and walked back.

"What sick guy?"

"Now that you mention it, I've heard one of your Rangers in there coughing sometimes. With the door locked and the lights off. I know the door was locked because I tried to open it once to see if the guy needed a cough drop or something."

As though to support his position, he dug into his pants pocket and pulled out a handful of Hall's cough drops, individually wrapped.

"Menthol flavor. They're the best ones. I like the flavor of the cherry ones, but they're really too sweet for me. Anyway, I have mild emphysema. Not enough to put me in bed and make me give up on life. But enough to give me occasional coughing spells. So I understand how your Ranger feels when he goes into a coughing fit and don't have anything to help control it.

"I've heard him coughing in there several times, but the one time I tried to go and offer him some relief, the door was locked. I knocked, but he didn't answer. Then I looked under the door and noticed the lights were off. I don't know why he preferred to work in the dark, but hey, that's none of my business. I'm just an old guy pushing a mop part time to supplement my social security check. What the hell do I know?"

"Did you ever see him come or go?"

"Can't recall. I don't pay a lot of attention to them that come and go around here. I do remember a Ranger named Waylor, used to work night shift. Nice man. Helped me boost my car one morning after I left my lights on all night. Ain't seen him in awhile, though. I think he may have quit."

"Yes, sir. He transferred to another Ranger company."

"Well, it wasn't him anyway."

"How do you know?"

"I never heard him cough. The guy in your office, I heard cough a lot of times. Plus, I've heard the cough coming from your office several times since Waylor stopped coming in. Anyway, you tell him to take care of that cough before it turns into something serious like emphysema or pneumonia or something."

"Do you know anything about the history of this area? What used to stand on this spot before this building was built?"

"Yeah, I was born in Abernathy a few miles away. My folks used to bring me into town on Saturday mornings to go the movies with my brother. God rest his soul. He's been gone for forty years now. Don't know how I've managed to outlive him for so long."

"Do you remember what used to be on this block when you were a kid?"

He paused to think for a minute.

"Let's see. On the west side there was a big Montgomery Ward building. Three stories. My brother and I used to run up and down the stairs, until one day I accidentally knocked a lady down. She wasn't hurt, but the stuff she was carrying went everywhere. Mother wouldn't let us go in there after that.

Just south of Montgomery Ward was the old newspaper building. The *Lubbock Avalanche-Journal*. I remember in the early days, when it was just the

Lubbock Avalanche. They didn't deliver to Abernathy in those days, but I remember at the front counter they kept a stack of each day's papers for the previous week. So Mother and Dad could go in there and pick and choose which days' paper they wanted to buy. It's a shame newspapers aren't what they used to be. The damn television and internet's puttin' 'em all outa business, you know."

"Yes, sir."

"Let's see. On the east side of the block was an old hotel. Big white wooden building, three stories as I recall. Can't remember the name of it. I remember they had a sandwich shop on the first floor and Donnie... he was my brother. Donnie and I used to go in there to get a cold bottle of pop and split a sandwich if we could talk Mother out of twenty cents. If we were broke we'd go in and look around for pennies on the floor and such. They had blowers on the first floor. Kind of an early swamp cooler. And on summer days it was a lot cooler in there than it was on the outside."

"It was called the Nicolett Hotel."

"Yeah, that's it. Like I said, when I used to go in it, her best days were behind her. She was patched together and on her last legs. But it was still a pretty impressive building, right across the street from the courthouse like it was."

"Did you ever hear of a man named Henry Jenkins?"

"No."

"He was a cowboy who died in that hotel. Of pneumonia. They say he died on the third floor, right around where our office is now. Said he coughed nonstop for days before he passed. He was the first man buried in the City of Lubbock Cemetery."

"I ain't never heard none of that. And he's got plenty of company out there at the cemetery now. Hell, I've got more relatives than I can count out there, pushing up daisies right alongside him. I'll be out there myself before long, I reckon.

"Say, are you saying that all the coughing I've heard belongs to a ghost?"

"Not necessarily. I'm just saying that no one has been in that office at night for the past two months."

The old man scratched his chin.

"Well, I'll be damned," the old man said, and went back to his mopping.

Chapter 39

"Randy, you told me the other day that you believe in ghosts. Have you ever actually seen one?"

"That's not what I said, Tom. I said there are a lot of things out there which are beyond our comprehension. Man believed the world was flat until just a few centuries ago. A hundred fifty years ago we believed the best way to cure cancer was to use leeches to suck it out of our bodies. And we still believe that you'll never find a date. Of course, that part's probably true."

"Very funny. Actually not so much."

"My point is, strange things happen all the time. Sometimes they can be explained away, but many times they can't. When we can't explain why or how something happened, then it's fair game for speculation. And I suppose that any theory is as good as another until it's proven wrong."

"I believe in ghosts."

Randy turned to look at him. Tom's comment surprised him. And it was obvious that he wanted to elaborate.

So Randy gave him the opportunity.

"Why? Have you seen one?"

"Yes. At least I think so. I was coming home late one night, from a job I had in high school. Flipping burgers at a burger joint in San Antonio. It was a school night, and I had to close that night because somebody on third shift didn't come in.

"So by the time we got everything counted and packed away and cleaned up it was after midnight. I was driving my high school piece of crap along Loop 1604, just a mile from home, when I passed this white figure walking along the shoulder. He was facing away from me, stooped over, and shuffling along like a little old lady. But he was too tall to be a lady, so I'm pretty sure it was a man.

"Anyway, there was just something about it that was strange. It was obviously a person, but I could see right through him. And there was something weird about his clothes. He wore like a robe or something. Pure white. And he kind of glowed.

"I slowed down as I passed him to get a better look, but at the same time I pulled into the other lane so he didn't walk in front of me.

"I wasn't scared at all. Just curious, really. Part of me wanted to stop to yell at him for walking along the highway so late at night. Part of me wanted to ask him if his car broke down, or if he needed help. And part of me just wanted to find out what he was all about.

"I should have just kept driving. I was tired from having worked so late, and it was a school night, and I was only gonna get about four hours of sleep. So I should have kept driving. But instead, I pulled over to the shoulder of the road. I watched the guy in my rear view mirror, maybe a hundred yards behind me and walking toward me.

"I as debating on what to say to him when he caught up to my car. But I never had to talk to him at all. I had my eyes locked on him, watching him walk as he got closer and closer. And then, while I was watching him, he just vaporized. Just faded away to nothing.

"Then I was finally scared. I burned rubber getting out of there.

"My dad was waiting up for me and asked me what happened. I was shaking like a leaf. I couldn't tell him. I didn't want him to think I was out drinking or something. I wanted to tell him, but I couldn't find the right words. So I just sat there, trying to process the whole thing.

"For some reason he thought I was upset because I was in an accident. I guess that's every parent's first assumption for their teenage son who's only been driving for a few months. He went out and inspected my car and came back and said there weren't any dents or anything.

"I couldn't tell him what happened until the next day. He said it was just fatigue that was causing me to hallucinate.

"But I don't care what he said. I saw what I saw. I don't know what the heck it was, and I've thought about that night a thousand times since then. But one thing I'm sure of, it wasn't a hallucination."

Tom sighed, as though he'd just relieved himself of a great burden he'd been carrying with him for a very long time.

He looked at Randy and said, "I know. You think I'm nuts, don't you?"

"Not at all, Tom. Not at all."

Chapter 40

The pair settled in and got comfortable. Randy busied himself reading Q. E. Terry's newest mystery, *Twisted Clues.*

Tom played a series of video games, headphones covering his ears. Randy glanced over at him, greatly amused by Tom's tendency to move his whole body in coordination with his hands on the game controller.

Randy shook his head and went back to his reading. As engrossed as Tom was with his games it was unlikely he'd hear a truck slamming into the side of the building. Much less a subtle sound made by a wayward spirit in the dead of the night.

But that was okay by Randy. It was still nice for Tom to come along. Even if he wasn't a lot of help, he was there to show his support. It was the way good partners were supposed to act.

The night came and went without incident.

As the sky started to lighten outside Randy got up and stood before the window. Across the street at the Lubbock County courthouse two uniformed sheriff's deputies were raising Old Glory on the courthouse lawn. Once the flag reached the top of the flagpole they stepped back, rendered a sharp salute, then did an about face and marched solemnly back into the courthouse.

Another day had begun.

The courts weren't in session today, but Randy was glad the city chose to honor the nation's flag on the weekends, instead of only on the days it was convenient to do so.

Randy watched the pigeons gather atop the gazebo on the courthouse lawn. His mind went back to 2007, when his best friend Todd Miller stood in the gazebo beside him. Todd was taking a mutual friend, Becky Morehouse, as his bride. Randy had been his best friend, and was therefore the logical choice to be his best man.

The memory was bittersweet. For as pleasant as it was it inevitably preceded his next memory. The memory of the night in 2009 when he was called to St. Mary's Hospital at three in the morning. Todd and a very pregnant Becky had been in a horrific collision involving an eighteen wheeler.

It was Randy who broke the news to Todd that Becky didn't make it. And neither did the baby.

Randy recalled how Todd's eyes just lost all semblance of life at the news. Within hours he was dead himself.

The autopsy report would say he died of internal injuries and blunt force trauma from the accident.

But Randy knew better. Randy knew that Todd had simply lost the desire to live after learning he'd lost his wife and child. He'd told his own body to give up. To shut down. To take him to a better place. He'd died of a broken heart, and a desire to rejoin his loved ones.

That experience had taught Randy about the frailty of life. And the power of the human mind.

"Hey partner."

It was Tom, finally pausing his video game and rejoining the real world.

"Hi Tom. Nice of you to join me."

"Hey, I figured you'd let me know if something happened. But you never raised the flag. Should I assume it was an uneventful night?"

"Yep. Not a creature was stirring, not a man nor a mouse."

"Great. Christmas in April."

"Did you win?"

"Oh, yeah. Several times over. But it's time to stop. Eight hours at the controller is long enough. I'm not a game fanatic, you know."

"Uh huh."

"Hey, I'm hungry. How about we give up this ghost hunt and go get some breakfast? You're buying."

"Why am I buying?"

"Stands to reason. You bought last time, so it's not my turn to buy."

"I'm not as sleepy as you think I am, pal."

"Then let's hang out here another hour. See if you're sleepier then."

"I thought you were hungry."

"I'm also a cheapskate. If I can get you to buy me breakfast by holding off another hour, I'll tough it out."

Randy sighed.

"I'll buy you breakfast, you tightwad. Let's go."

They straightened up a bit and gathered their things.

Tom asked, "So, you didn't hear anything? Nothing at all?"

"Not a thing."

As they walked toward the door, though, they heard what sounded like a man groaning. Followed by a series of raspy coughs.

The men looked at each other. Randy's face showed a sense of calm curiosity.

Tom's face went pale. As though he'd seen a ghost.

Or at least heard one.

Their office door opened into the hallway on the office's west end. The noises appeared to come from the east side of the office suite.

They slowly made their way to the area where the sound seemed to originate, being perfectly silent as they went and listening for more sounds.

On the east side of the suite, they heard more coughing. This time to the west of them.

They returned to the office door, where they paused and waited for a full five minutes.

They heard nothing else.

"What did it sound like to you?"

"Ten frickin' children on a playground singing *Ring Around the Rosie*, Randy. You know darn well what it sounded like. It sounded like a dead cowboy named

Jenkins coughing his lungs out. Tell me that's not what you heard."

"No. That's pretty much what I heard too. I can't explain how, but that's a good description of it."

"So what are you gonna tell the major?"

"I'm going to tell him exactly what we heard. We'll let him decide what to do about it. I know what I'm going to recommend to him though."

"Yeah? What's that?"

Randy turned to him and gave him a huge smile while locking the office door.

"I'm going to suggest that we reinstitute a night shift. And that he put you on Waylor's old shift."

"Very funny. I'll buy you breakfast if you don't."

"Deal."

Chapter 41

Randy was exhausted. It had been a long and trying week. He'd spent most of it tying up loose ends in one of the biggest narcotics manufacturing busts in the history of the Northern Division. They'd shut down an operation that was putting six kilograms of crystal poison on Texas streets each and every day.

Randy was amazed at the aftermath of such an operation. The initial arrests were made and all the reports were filed. But that was only the tip of the iceberg.

In a case such as this, some of the arrestees always make deals. In this case in particular, because of the new tactic of tacking on racketeering charges, there were more requests for plea deals than ever before. Also, word got around that the cartel had planted a hitman, or enforcer, within their ranks to silence any snitches.

It was a major mistake. For it had the reverse affect. Instead of silencing those who wanted to turn state's evidence, it created more of them. The rank and file workers were incensed. And their tongues were loosened. Especially when they were looking at thirty year prison sentences.

Of course, each time a suspect made a plea deal, he had to name names. And those additional suspects had to be rounded up. Since this was a big time manufacturing operation, they didn't deal with no-name street dealers. They dealt with the next step up in the food chain. The distributers who took the dope from the lab to those dealers.

Those people tended to deal in greater quantities than the street level dealers, who usually only had a couple of grams or eight-balls on them at any given time.

These middle men were frequently taken down with several times that much.

And greater quantities meant they were looking at harsher sentences. Which meant their tongues were loosened even more.

One of the federal agents whistled at the number of suspects who were lining up to provide additional names and lighten their sentences.

He jokingly likened it to a Bible passage. "Roundup one gave us twenty suspects. Those twenty suspects begat twenty more, which begat twenty more still. And the world was a better place without them."

With each additional group of suspects, warrants had to be issued. A takedown team had to be organized so the warrants could be served. Evidence had to be gathered. New suspects had to be questioned. The district attorney had to be consulted. Deals had to be made to generate another list of names.

All of this, of course, crated a mountain of paperwork.

Randy's part of the operation and its aftermath were done now, except for the testifying. That would take place here and there over the course of several months. Before he and Tom were given a bit of time off, they'd already logged more than sixty hours in this particular week.

And that was before they'd stayed up all night long waiting for signs of a ghost.

A ghost who perhaps toyed with them, making them wait until the very last minute to present itself.

He wondered about the sounds they'd heard. He knew they weren't hallucinating. They'd heard the same thing.

He knew it wasn't some hidden tape recorder left behind by a prankster Ranger who'd heard of their planned mission that night.

Because the sounds seemed to move around the suite of offices as they did.

He'd have time to wonder more about that later. When his head was clearer. When he wasn't so drained after coming down off the adrenaline rush that had carried him through the first part of his week.

Randy looked at the piece of paper on his night table.

Sarah 548-6708 Call me cowboy.

When she handed it to him he read it and cracked a joke.

"You want me to call you cowboy? How come?"

She laughed. That was his intent. It was an easy laugh. Her smile was genuine, not forced. And he decided she was most beautiful when she smiled.

He'd found that most women weren't willing to wait until he retired from the Rangers to start a serious relationship.

And that was understandable. He knew they had things like maternal goals and biological clocks and sensitive feelings and all that stuff.

But he was adamant. He felt strongly that the men in his family were living on borrowed time. Several of them had been injured on the job, but none ever died.

He felt the odds were against him. That perhaps he would finally be the one unlucky enough to fall and not get up again.

Some of his friends thought him crazy. Major Shultz thought it was a dangerous outlook for a Ranger to have. Perhaps even a self-fulfilling destiny. But Randy had assured him, it wouldn't cause him to be less careful. It wouldn't cause him to take risks on the job that others wouldn't. That he shouldn't.

"If anything it'll make me more cautious," Randy had told him. "I more than anyone want to prove myself wrong. I want to serve my ten years and then retire this badge once and for all. I'll give it back to Wilford P.

And then I'll settle down and have the rest of my life to have babies and raise a family."

There had been several women who tried to convince him his plan was folly.

Randy's dad once told him the main difference in men and women when it came to relationships.

"Men tend to search until they find the perfect woman. Then they marry her hoping she will not change. Women, on the other hand, tend to settle. They know that all men are flawed. They settle for one who is not perfect, thinking they can change them."

Perhaps *that* was Randy's self-fulfilling destiny. For in his experience, his father was right on the money. Or maybe Randy just kept stumbling across women who fit his father's description.

In any event, there were several women in Randy's past who'd fallen for him. After all, he was a tall and handsome cowboy with impeccable morals in a world where that was increasingly rare.

"I love you, but I can't wait forever," they'd say. "I know the risks. I know I could end up a widow. I know our children could be left without a father. I'm willing to risk it. You should too." Trying to change him. Trying to change his timeline.

Randy had never changed his original game plan, and had broken some hearts.

Sarah gave no indication that she was any different. She didn't give him the impression she was someone who'd fall head over heels for him. He merely got the sense she was a fun and carefree woman, full of life and wanting to experience everything the world had to offer.

Perhaps including Randy.

But then again, that's how the other women started out as well.

He'd call her and make plans to see her again.

He'd get to know her and become her friend. He'd wine her and dine her and take her on picnics and to amusement parks. They'd go riding and swimming together. They'd stay up late at night, sharing the ups and down of their lives, as well as their hopes and dreams.

And he'd tell her two things.

First of all, that she shouldn't fall for him. Because he would not, could not, consider a serious relationship until his service with the Rangers was done.

Second, that his mind was made up. He might be crazy. He might be stubborn. He might be a hard-headed old mule. But he would not be swayed by a beautiful girl or any of her charms. This, as he saw it, was his destiny. He would fulfill it. Then, if he survived, he would move onto other things.

As before, he'd be perfectly honest with Sarah. And he'd let her make the choice whether she wanted to hang around and wait.

But that was all tomorrow, and in the days ahead.

Today, after being up all night ghost-hunting, he was beat.

He was sound asleep mere moments after his head hit the pillow.

Chapter 42

Randy slept fitfully that night.

He dreamed about a young cowboy, lying in a bed all alone as he slowly died from a dreadful sickness. How it must have felt knowing he'd soon be gone. Wondering if anyone would grieve for him. Whether anyone would miss him.

He dreamed about Sarah Anna Speer. He wondered who she was, where she'd come from. Whether she'd be the one to finally accept his terms and to become his friend for the next seven years. Then perhaps more after that.

He dreamed again about an incredible calamity enveloping the earth. He dreamed of great famine, and violence, and loss of hope.

In his dream, his mother came to him and tried to explain the visions.

"They can be a blessing," she said. "But also a curse. Especially when you know something is coming, but you cannot stop it and you cannot share any details of it. One of the worst things you'll ever have to do is to hold a dear friend and tell them things you only know a little bit about. You'll tell them that someone close to them will die. But you won't know who, or when, or how.

"You'll fool yourself, Randy, into thinking you're doing that friend some good. That you're making it easier on them. In reality, you're just adding to their torment, by making them wonder. By making them take all their loved ones under their wings and trying to find a way to stop the unstoppable.

"But you have to tell them. Even knowing the additional stress and pain you'll cause them, you can't *not* tell them.

"Because deep down inside you understand they have a right to know.

"Having the visions is something you'll learn to live with. But you'll also come to hate them."

It was at those words that Randy stirred, although he didn't open his eyes for several minutes.

He'd set his alarm for three p.m.

He didn't want to sleep the day away, for fear he wouldn't be sleepy at his normal bedtime. Yet he needed to get a few hours in or he wouldn't be functional in the waning hours of the day.

Three p.m. seemed the perfect compromise. It would give him some of the sleep his weary body craved, yet still give him enough hours in the day to do the things he needed to do. And would ensure he was still tired enough at the end of the day to get a restful night's sleep.

His plan was to arise at three and take an afternoon jog through the streets of west Lubbock, then shower and do some grocery shopping.

He was still debating whether or not to call Sarah.

He knew there was an unwritten rule against calling a girl the day after you met her. His friends had always told him that.

"You don't want to appear to be needy or desperate," they always said. "You need to make her feel that she needs you more than you need her."

It wasn't until he'd dated for a while that he learned that girls give the exact same advice to their girlfriends. The whole first phone call thing was therefore a kind of dating Mexican standoff. Randy wondered how many potentially great relationships never got off the ground because neither party wanted to be the first to make that call, and they drifted in opposite directions because of it.

He'd make the call, but he'd wait until the following day. When he was caught up on his sleep. That way he wouldn't say something stupid, and ruin any chance he'd having of dating Sarah.

In his mind's eye he could still see her. Tall, beautiful, sweet and funny.

It might be hard this time to keep his eye on his plan and keep her at arm's length.

But he would. He was that devoted to his future. And to hers, if fate lead them in that direction.

He finally opened his eyes and looked at the clock.

He wanted to see if he had enough time to snooze before the alarm went off.

But the clock was dark.

Chapter 43

The apartment Randy called home was well-maintained but old. Nestled between Lubbock Christian University and the six-lane loop which surrounded the city, the complex was built in the very early days of the 1960s.

Like most complexes built in that era it was made to last, with sturdy materials and quality craftsmanship not common by today's standards. The apartment was still going strong, and would last another fifty years or more.

Unless a tornado blew it away before then.

Still, things are prone to wearing out, since nothing lasts forever.

Randy had been having a problem in recent months with the wiring in the building. There were frequent power outages, and the electricians called in by apartment maintenance has been unable to locate the problem.

"A short somewhere in the wiring," was as close as they'd been able to find and to fix the problem.

The outages were usually short, and required only that Randy go to his breaker box and reset the main breaker switch.

And it was no big deal, really. He had to get up to get a drink of water anyway. And he wanted to go for an afternoon run.

He went to the breaker box and opened it, then reset the top switch. He expected to hear the air conditioner blower come to life and the refrigerator start humming.

He heard neither.

He reached behind him and flipped the overhead light on in the hallway.

Nothing.

"Well, I'll be…" he muttered to himself as he tried the reset two more times.

Still nothing.

It wasn't the end of the world. It was daytime, so the lights weren't a problem. Hot water for his shower wouldn't be a problem either, since it was heated by natural gas.

In all likelihood it was temporary. A transformer may have blown atop a power pole, or maybe an out-of-control car took the pole itself out.

Lubbock Power and Light was usually pretty good about identifying the problem and getting service restored quickly.

He put on his running gear, then picked up his cell phone to check the time on it.

It was dead.

That was odd. Then he remembered that he'd been up all night, the phone in his pocket. He couldn't plug it in to charge all night as was his normal practice.

No sense taking it along on his run. It wouldn't do him any good dead, and he couldn't charge it until the power came back on.

He did the next best thing.

He put the phone on his night table and plugged it in. With any luck, the power would be restored while he was out running, and his phone would have the beginnings of a good charge by the time he returned.

He picked up his Dad's old watch, which he treasured, and which still kept perfect time. Provided he remembered to wind it every day.

Luckily he'd wound it in the wee hours of the morning as he waited for Henry Jenkins to make his presence known.

The watch said 2:20 p.m.

He'd awakened a bit earlier than he'd planned. But that wasn't a major problem. It would just make him sleep that much more restfully when he retired later.

He walked to the living room, checked his resting pulse, and stretched.

Then he went to one knee, retied his left shoelace, and grabbed a bottle of water from his refrigerator.

The water was still cold. He estimated the power hadn't been off for more than an hour or two.

Randy walked out into a beautiful day. Not a cloud in sight, and blue skies that seemed to stretch forever. It would be a great day for a three mile run.

Only his run would have to wait.

In the parking lot just outside his front door was old Mrs. Swenson, one of Randy's neighbors and friends.

Randy was far too polite to ask the woman her age, but she was eighty if she was a day.

Fiercely independent as women of her generation were prone to be, she lived alone, still drove herself everywhere she needed to go. Still carried her own groceries, and resisted any offers to help her.

With everything except cars. Cars baffled her.

Chapter 44

Mrs. Swenson drove a 1963 Ford Galaxie 500, in near mint condition.

Her son David and his wife bought the car for her some years before. It seemed that Mrs. Swenson had an affection from things from her early days, when life was less rushed and simpler.

One of her favorite television shows was *The Andy Griffith Show*. It was old, as she was, and in black and white. Or, as she liked to put it, "lighter and darker shades of gray, like me."

She confided in Randy once that the main reason she enjoyed the show was that Aunt Bea reminded her so much of her own mother, God rest her soul, who'd been gone for many years.

David bought her the car because it supposedly was used as a prop on the set of the show. Its previous owner produced a letter of authenticity from a long-gone studio in Hollywood that claimed Don Knotts, who played the Barney Fife character, had driven the car in four episodes.

There was no way to confirm or deny the claim, and David had paid a premium price for the car based upon it. But he didn't care. She was tickled pink to get the car, and he'd made her happy.

"That's what's important to me," he said. "She's the only mother I have, and I won't have her forever. I want to make her as happy as I can in her last years. I owe her that much."

On this particular afternoon, as Randy emerged from his apartment for his three mile run, Mrs. Swenson wasn't very happy. Not at all.

There she was, gazing beneath the raised hood of the old Ford, scanning every inch of the engine and muttering under her breath.

She was a sweet old lady, Randy knew. She'd brought him home-baked cookies and pies on several occasions, and chicken soup when he was under the weather.

But bless her heart, she didn't know beans about cars. She'd confessed to him before that she wouldn't know a carburetor from a battery cable.

But by God, she knew what a hubcap was, she'd said.

And now here she was, clueless yet no less independent, trying to figure out on her own why her car wouldn't start.

"Hello, Mrs. Swenson. Having problems?"

"Oh hello, Randy. Yes. It won't start. Won't do anything."

"Here. Let me take a look at it."

Randy stuck his own head under the hood to look around.

The engine compartment of a 1963 Ford was remarkably simple. There were no emission control systems competing for space. No endless array of hoses and wires and cables twisting and turning every which way. There were the basic components and they were spaced around the compartment in a manner which provided convenient working space between them. On each side of the engine block Randy could look down and see the ground beneath the car.

Engines were much simpler back in 1963.

The first thing he noticed was the smell. Like wiring burning. And a slightly acidic scent.

Then he saw the positive battery cable. It was fried and melted and blackened.

"I'm afraid it looks like your battery shorted out. I can take you to get a new one. Can you wait until after I get back from my run?"

"Oh, I don't want to burden you, dear. I tried to call David, but my telephone isn't working either. Because of the power outage, I suppose. I guess I'm going to break down and get myself one of those cellular things, or whatever you call them."

"A cell phone. Yes, ma'am."

"David and Stacey, they tell me I'm the only person on the face of the earth you doesn't have one. And I see children in the supermarket all the time, and even they have them. So I guess I'm going to have to break down and get myself one.

"I'm just not one for newfangled gadgets. I like things that are old, like me."

"Yes, ma'am," Randy said noncommittally as he closed the hood. "I'll tell you what. Let me go for my run and get a quick shower. That'll take maybe forty five minutes or so. Then if David's not here to rescue you by then, we'll run up to Walmart and get a new battery and cable for you and I'll put them on. Fair enough?"

"Thank you, Randy. You're a doll."

Randy didn't have a chance to respond before both of them were distracted by the very loud screams of a woman, coming from a couple of apartment buildings to their west.

Chapter 45

Randy was off like a shot, leaving a bewildered Mrs. Swenson in the parking lot as he darted around the corner of the building.

He instinctively reached for the service weapon on the right side of his belt, even knowing it wasn't there. One of the few times he left it on his dresser was during his daily run. He hoped he wouldn't need it, but there was simply no time to go back after it.

The woman's screams turned to a loud wail by the time he found her, a baby in her arms and a three year old looking sadly up at her from an umbrella stroller.

Another neighbor had beaten him there and was already trying to console the woman.

"I'm a peace officer, ma'am. Are you okay?"

She was a mess, but managed to nod her head up and down.

"Tell me what happened."

"He stole my purse. The bastard stole my purse. We were just walking up to the store to get some flashlight batteries and some water, and he came out of nowhere and grabbed my purse and…"

Randy didn't need the long version, and interrupted her.

"What did he look like and which way did he go?"

She sniffled once before continuing.

"A white guy. A teenager. Blue jeans and blue shirt."

She pointed between two other buildings to indicate which direction he'd run in.

"I couldn't chase him because of my babies…"

Randy told the neighbor, "Please call 911. Get the police out here."

Then he once again disappeared around the corner of the building, in hot pursuit.

Randy never found the robber. He'd disappeared into one of the dozens of apartments in the complex, or in the other apartment complexes which covered the block and every block surrounding it. In all likelihood he was at that moment rifling through the purse, pulling out whatever cash he could find to buy cigarettes, booze or drugs. The items which were no use to him would likely end up in a nearby dumpster.

But Randy found something else he'd never bargained for. Something which caused him to momentarily forget about the robber, the purse, the victim.

He was on the outer perimeter of the apartments now, on their west side. The side which fronted Loop 289.

"The loop," as it was called in Lubbock, ran for twenty seven miles and completely encircled the city. Normally at this time of day it was bustling as hundreds of drivers used it to quickly get from one part of town to another while skirting the traffic lights and stop signs.

But not today.

Randy looked at the loop in awe and began walking slowly toward it.

What he saw reminded him of a disaster movie.

No. A television show. A hit show about zombies in the city of Atlanta.

He saw no zombies. But what he saw was reminiscent of a scene from the show's opening credits. A scene which showed I-75 north of Atlanta, strewn with broken down and abandoned vehicles.

Loop 289 looked like a parking lot. There were stalled cars everywhere, in every lane. Most had their hoods up. People were milling about, conferring in small groups. Many had their heads stuck under their hoods, examining their engines. Much like Randy had been doing with Mrs. Swenson's old Ford just a few minutes before.

He looked around him. Took a really good look, for the first time.

The access road and the entry and exit ramps were clogged with stalled cars in the same manner. So were the surface streets which surrounded the apartment complex on its other three sides.

Randy looked around, greatly confused.

And he had a sour feeling in the pit of his stomach.

He remembered his dream. His mother's warning. Her premonitions were seldom specific. Neither were his, on the rare occasions he'd had one. But the latest premonition, the one waking him up at night, told him that a catastrophe was coming. Perhaps the biggest catastrophe ever to hit mankind.

He began to feel ill.

But then he caught himself. He'd gone off on a mission to catch a thief and had failed. His first order of business was to assist the victim as best he could. Then he'd try to figure out whatever was happening and why all the cars suddenly stopped working.

He trudged back to the hapless victim, who by now had stopped crying and attracted a small crowd.

She looked at him expectantly as he approached, but he had to shake his head and tell her, "I'm sorry, ma'am. No sign of him."

The woman he'd given instructions to call the police said, "We can't call 911, officer. Nobody's cell phones are working either."

It wasn't just the cars. It wasn't just the phones. It wasn't a local power outage. It was spread wider than anyone could possibly imagine.

It was catastrophic.

Randy apologized again for being unable to help the woman.

"What apartment are you in, ma'am?"

"Apartment two twenty."

"He'll probably take all of your cash and credit cards out of your purse and throw the rest into the dumpster. I'll dig through the dumpsters in the area he ran to tomorrow. Maybe we can at least find your driver's license and personal things. When we can get ahold of the police, give them a good description of the thief. They may know him if he's done this kind of thing before, and may know where he lives."

It wasn't the answer she was looking for. But she sensed that Randy really had tried to help her, and had done all he could do at the moment.

"Thank you."

"You're welcome, ma'am. If I can find anything in the dumpster tomorrow, I'll bring it to you."

He walked away dejected. He enjoyed helping people. It was why he was a Ranger. And he felt as though he'd let her down.

Chapter 46

The hours that followed the blackout were chaotic beyond compare.

It being Saturday, Randy knew there was no need to rush back to his office. The Rangers normally shut down their local detachment on the weekends, unless they were working a special case. Or unless they were recalled. And that didn't seem likely.

They did have a pyramid recall system in place. It was laid out on a diagram on a sheet of paper Randy carried in the back of his wallet.

The pyramid got its name from the format, and was patterned after a similar recall roster used by the military for decades.

At the top center of the page, the very top of the pyramid, was the name "Major John C. Shultz, Company C Commander." Beneath the name were the major's home and cell phone numbers and address.

Below his were the names and information of his two lieutenants. Below them were the Rangers in the company, lined up nice and neat.

The concept was simple. In the event of a state or national emergency, the Major had the option of implementing a recall, meaning all the men in his company would report immediately to work to do what they could to help in the situation.

To implement the recall, the major need only call the two lieutenants beneath him on the roster and tell them a recall was in effect.

Each lieutenant would immediately call the person below him on the roster and pass along the same instructions. Then they would dress quickly and report to work.

Each successive man in line would do the same thing, until every man on the roster was notified and on his way. If one of the men could not be contacted, he would be skipped over and the person beneath him would be contacted instead. In that manner, one or two men might be missing, but the chain would not be broken.

The Texas Rangers' standard was for all men to be notified within ten minutes. And for all of them to report to work within thirty.

It was a system which worked well.

But there were a couple of major problems with it.

The primary choice of notification was home phone, then cell phone, in that order.

Of late, many of the Rangers had their home phones disconnected. They were following a national trend and thinking, hey, they had their cell phones with them twenty four seven. Why did they even need a home phone? So they had their service disconnected to save money.

No one ever thought to consider what chaos might ensue if none of the cell phones worked.

At the bottom of the recall roster, below the pyramid, were a set of brief instructions on how the system would work.

Item six stated, *Call the man listed immediately below you before reporting for duty. If for any reason you cannot reach him by phone, call the person after him. Then go to the uncontacted Ranger's home to alert him before you report.*

The team which designed the roster thought they'd covered all the bases.

But in a case where none of the phones worked, everybody would have to be contacted in person.

And in a case where none of the vehicles worked either, that would be next to impossible.

Every effort was made to arrange the Rangers on the roster somewhat geographically. So that should a Ranger have to go to someone's house to notify him, he wouldn't have to drive all the way across town to do it.

But still, there were typically several miles of space between any of the men in the company, and no good way to cover that ground in the interim. And at least three of the Rangers, Randy knew, didn't even live in Lubbock. Two of them, brothers, lived in nearby Woodrow. The other commuted from Sweetwater each day.

Randy decided to do what in his mind was most logical. He'd do what he could to help his neighbors who were in most need. Then he'd make his way to the federal building in downtown Lubbock, some seven miles or so. He would assume the other Rangers in his company would do the same thing.

Once there, Major Shultz or the ranking lieutenant would give them their marching orders.

Randy returned to the parking lot in front of his apartment to find that old Mrs. Swenson had retreated inside.

He knocked on her door.

"Hello, Randy. Is everything okay over there? Was the woman hurt?"

"No, ma'am. Only angry. Someone stole her purse and got away, I'm afraid. Are you doing okay?"

"Yes. Do you know of any way I can get ahold of David?"

"No, ma'am. I'm afraid I don't. But he and Stacey only live a few miles from here. Is David still off on the weekends?"

"Yes."

"My guess is that he'll find a way to make it over here, even if he has to walk, to make sure you're okay. This blackout may last awhile. It looks like it's city wide and of a nature they've never had to deal with before."

"Oh, my."

"Do you have enough provisions to get you by? Bottled water? Food? Medicine?"

"I don't have any bottled water. I usually use tap water. But I just turned on the faucet and it's only coming out at a trickle."

"The power outage has probably shut down the pumps at the water plant. What's left in the pipes may not be safe to drink. I've got bottled water at my place. I'll bring over a case for you. I wouldn't drink the tap water.

"How about medicine and food?"

"I've got plenty of medicine for a couple of weeks, and my cupboards are full."

"Okay. I'm going to bring over the water and then leave you alone. I've got to get to the office to find out how I can help out. After I bring you the water I want you to lock yourself in your apartment. Don't open the door for anyone except for David when he gets here. He'll take good care of you when he arrives. You just hang in there until then, okay?"

"Randy... what's causing this? Is it bad?"

"I'm afraid I don't know what's causing it, ma'am. But yes. I think it's very very bad."

Chapter 47

Ranger Randy, as he was known around the neighborhood, spent the next half hour walking door to door, trying to soothe the fears of his neighbors. At the same time he was advising them on how best to deal with the situation.

"Watch out for the vulnerable. The old folks and the single moms. We don't know how long this blackout is going to last. If it goes into the night, there's a good chance there will be looters out after darkness. Maybe home invaders too, but my guess is that they'll hit the supermarkets and convenience stores first.

"Stay indoors and protect yourselves. As I said, if you have an elderly neighbor or someone else who's vulnerable, invite them to stay the night with you. It'll be to your mutual benefit.

"I know the faucets are still dripping. Catch it, but don't drink it. Save it in case you run out of other water, and then drink it only if you have to. And boil it for ten minutes before you do.

"Don't waste your drinking water to clean yourselves. It's too valuable. Protect your water like it was the most valuable possession you own. Because if this thing lasts for more than a few days, it may well be.

"Above all else, band together and protect each other."

Randy knew he needed to get downtown. He was stalling for as long as he could waiting for his partner, Tom Cohen, to arrive. Tom was directly above Randy on the pyramid roster. It was Tom's duty to notify Randy in case of recall or national emergency. If he couldn't reach Randy by phone, he was supposed to drive to Randy's house to notify him.

There were no recall procedures for a situation where there were no vehicles. But Randy had faith in his partner. Tom would find a way to get to him.

And he did.

By bicycle.

It brought the first smile to Randy's face all day.

"Hello, partner. I didn't even know you had a bike."

"Of course I have a bike. I thought everyone did. I just seldom use mine. It had a flat. I had to take the tube out and patch it, or I'd have been here sooner.

"I've contacted you. Who are you supposed to contact?"

Randy shook his head. "Nobody. I'm the new kid on the block, remember? I'm at the end of the list."

"Well then, I guess we head downtown. Do you have your own bike?"

"Nope. I guess I'll have to jog it. It's twice my normal run, but I think the adrenaline will get me there."

Randy turned to see David Swenson running up the sidewalk, obviously in distress. David was a big man, and obviously out of shape. He looked as though he were getting ready to have a heart attack.

"Hey, David. Slow down there. Are you okay?"

He had to stop and catch his breath before he could speak.

"Yes. Just need to check on mom."

"I just left her. She's fine."

"Randy, what in hell is going on?"

Randy winced, just a bit. But it was enough to remind his friend that he didn't like that particular word.

"Sorry. What's going on? Have the Rangers told you guys anything?"

"I don't know, my friend. We're headed downtown to find out what we can, and to get instructions from our company commander. Are you going to stay here tonight?"

"Yes. My two sons are home. They can protect Stacey. I'll stay here until the lights come back on and protect mom."

Randy had a bad feeling in his gut that the lights wouldn't be back on for a very long time. But he kept that thought to himself. The situation was stressful enough on all of them.

Randy looked to Tom and said, "I'm ready, partner."

"Good. Hand me your backpack."

Randy's pack didn't contain much. His service weapon and wallet, four bottles of water, and a Subway meatball sandwich he'd bought the day before and left in the fridge. He handed the pack to Tom, who threw it over his own.

"I'll wait for you at 19th and Slide and we'll trade off."

"Sounds good."

Randy smiled as Tom rode away. He was coming to know his partner quite well, and he'd suspected Tom would insist on sharing his wheels.

In the early twentieth century the Lubbock city planners laid out the street grid in perfect one mile blocks. Each line on the grid marked a main thoroughfare. Those were the streets zoned for businesses, and were a bit wider to allow for additional traffic.

Residential streets were set between the main thoroughfares. They were designed for lighter traffic and were narrower.

Now, a hundred years later, one traveling across the city could still gauge his distance between stop lights on the main thoroughfares. The distance between Randy's apartment and the intersection of 19th Street and Slide Road was exactly one mile.

It was an easy jog for Randy, who was used to running every afternoon.

He found Tom waiting at the intersection, as promised.

"I put my backpack inside of yours to make them easier to carry. I also ate your sandwich."

Randy knew he was joking.

But he had a comeback.

After he put his pack back on his own back and wheeled away on Tom's bike, he called over his shoulder, "Hope you enjoyed the sandwich. See you downtown."

Then he cackled like an old witch.

But Tom knew better. Tom jogged exactly one mile, to the intersection of 19th Street and Quaker Avenue. He found Randy straddling his bike on the street corner and sipping from a bottle of water.

"Two guys came from different directions and asked if they could borrow my bike for a minute, then bring it back."

Tom laughed.

"That's nothing. I had one guy run me down with five hundred dollar bills in his hand He wanted to buy the thing."

The bicycle had become a commodity more precious than gold or silver. But they didn't loan it out and couldn't sell it. They needed it to get downtown to Company C's headquarters.

Chapter 48

The sun was starting to get low in the western sky when Tom pulled his bike up to the Mahon Federal Building in downtown Lubbock.

He stopped to smoke a cigarette and to catch his breath.

He'd known even before playing bicycle leapfrog across the streets of Lubbock that he wasn't in the best of shape.

Now, as he waited for Randy to finish the last leg of his run and catch up to him, he resolved to do two things: stop smoking once and for all, and get to the gym at least three nights a week.

Of course, those were the same resolutions he'd made on each of the three previous new years. But this time he really meant it.

Just like he did the previous three new years.

He could see Randy's tiny figure, some two blocks away now. He could go on in. Major Shultz was already upstairs. He knew because he could see the major's car, parked in one of the *Law Enforcement Only* slots on the north side of the building. He wondered how in the world he managed to get it started, when every other car they'd seen was as dead as a brick.

Yes, he could go upstairs. But Randy was his partner. They'd become best friends and had been through thick and thin together. They were not unlike an old married couple in that respect. They had each other's backs. And whatever had caused this, and no matter how bad it got, they'd face it together.

Randy too was out of breath when he climbed the steps to the federal building.

"I wonder how the major got his car started."

"Yeah. I was wondering the same thing. You need a minute?"

"No, I'm okay. Let's get up there and see what this is all about."

Tom snuffed his cigarette out against the building's wall and asked, "Do you think anybody will mind if I bring this in?"

Randy looked around at the near-empty parking lot.

"I don't think there's anybody here *to* mind, Tom. And if you leave it out here, somebody's sure to steal it. Better take it in."

The pair expected emergency lights to be on in the building. They expected to hear the quiet hum of the huge generator contained in the basement. They tested it once a month by taking the power down and then firing up the generator to keep it sound. Everyone in the building knew the sound it made and the way the walls vibrated when it was running.

But today it wasn't running. The emergency lighting in the hallways was completely dead.

So was the cypher lock outside the door of the Ranger's office. Randy dug out his key and opened the door the old fashioned way.

"I'm glad you brought yours," Tom said. "I left my keys at home."

"How are you gonna get back in?"

"My girlfriend's there."

"I thought you were between girlfriends."

"The last one came back."

"Good for you."

"We'll see."

They expected, as long as it took for them to get there, to find the office full of other Rangers.

Instead, they found Major John Shultz, the Company C Commander, and Stan Davis, one of the Rangers assigned to Hale County.

It was hard to disguise the worried look on Major Shultz's face.

"Good evening, Rangers. Thanks for making it in."

"Sorry it took us so long, sir. How did you get your car started?"

"I didn't. I was already here when the power went out. Trying to catch up on my paperwork. I was getting ready to leave when everything started popping. There were little puffs of smoke here and there, and the smell of electrical wires burning. My cell phone popped, and then was completely dead.

"My car's as dead as everyone else's. I took a bunch of keys down to the fleet vehicle lot. They're dead too. Every single one of them.

"I don't know what this is all about, boys. But I've got the feeling it's big. Real big. And I've got the feeling it's gonna last awhile too."

Tom asked him, "Sir, what are our orders?"

"Sit down, Tom. You're pale and sweating. Did you run all the way here?"

"Only half the way, sir. Randy and I took turns on my bike."

"Randy, you sit down too. Stan here thinks we've been attacked. Stan, do you want to explain?"

Stan turned to the others.

"I sat in on a Homeland Security threat assessment briefing not long ago. Remember, we got an invitation to attend their conference in Austin and none of you other guys wanted to go?

"Well, anyway, I think it's North Korea. Homeland Security was going over all the possible threats we face as a nation, from Al Qaeda to ISIS to Russia to North Korea.

"It turns out that if you take a nuclear warhead and explode it high over a foreign country, it can knock out the power grid and all the communications networks for the country or countries beneath it. All the power stations, all the generators, all the cell towers. Homeland Security said that crazy fool who runs North Korea has been developing nuclear warheads and a delivery system and they thought that was his eventual goal."

Tom said, "It's a good theory. But wouldn't we have seen something? A mushroom cloud in the sky or something? We almost certainly would have heard a blast. I mean, I've never been near a nuclear bomb when it detonates, but I would guess it's pretty noisy. Even way up in the sky."

"Maybe. Maybe not. Who can say? I mean, we're on unfamiliar territory here. Nothing like this has ever happened before, to my knowledge. We don't know whether this is just the first step in a major attack. We don't know how far it spreads. Whether it's just this area or nationwide. Heck, for all we know this could be the beginning of a war between the worlds. Maybe we've been attacked by some kind of alien weapon that can wipe out our technology without hurting any people."

"Whatever it is, it's ugly. And it's likely to get much uglier."

Chapter 49

Around sunset the four Rangers abandoned their office. It was pitch black and there were no lanterns or other means of providing light, save Tom's cigarette lighter. It being a government building, all flames were strictly forbidden. Not even a decorative candle was allowed.

Randy was able to find a flashlight in the back of one of his desk drawers, but it was dead.

The major sent Stan out to dig through the trunks of all the fleet vehicles for more flashlights or batteries. Every single one he found was dead.

Once out of their office, they gathered on the front steps of the federal building and waited for the other Rangers to come trickling in.

By midnight everyone had made it in.

"Okay," the major began. "I don't have to tell any of you that we're in a world of hurt. You can see that with your own eyes. We don't know what we're dealing with, and even if we did we don't have any instructions regarding how to deal with it. I'm afraid we're going lone wolf, until such time as we can establish communications with HQ in Austin and get our assignments."

The ten men of Company C were huddled close. They had to be, to see one another's faces and know who was saying what. There was a full moon in the sky, but it was partially hidden by clouds. What resulted was a group of dimly lit faces, downtrodden every one, speaking in somber tones about their worst fears.

It wasn't a pleasant place to be.

The major continued.

"Right now, as I see it, our main job is to help the city prevent panic and to protect the citizens of Lubbock against those who would do them harm. At least that's our mission until Austin gives us another one. I've got a couple of ideas on how we might contact HQ. That's what I'll be working on the next couple of days. In the meantime, it is imperative we stay in contact.

"Keep track of your days, boys. Today is the eighth day of the month. Two days from now, on the tenth, I want to reassemble here at high noon. Hopefully we'll have instructions from HQ by then. Hopefully we'll have more information on how widespread this thing is. At the very least, we can share information between ourselves about what's going on out there and how best to help the citizens of Lubbock survive it.

"Lieutenant Gomez, I want you to ride your bike out to the stable. I know it'll take you several hours. Take your time, don't give yourself a heart attack. Tell the stableman that over the next day or two all of my Rangers are going to come out and pick up a horse. Have him keep track of which one goes to who. Those ponies will be assigned to you and will be your responsibilities. You are to take good care of them. They may be your only source of transportation for the foreseeable future."

"We're returning to horseback?"

"We have no choice."

"But sir... how will we feed them? We live in the city. There's no feed stores... no hay."

"No, but there are city parks and playa lakes within five blocks of you, wherever you are in the city. The city of Lubbock gives me a citation every time I go more than six days without mowing my lawn. But the grass in the city parks is usually knee high. That's because the city values my money more than my park participation. Well now we're gonna use that to our advantage. The grass is plenty high for our horses to graze. That's where they'll eat."

"Yes, sir."

"The rest of you... go back to your homes. Tomorrow make your way to the stable and pick up your ponies. Then do what you can to help the community. Be back here at noon two days from now. I hope to have instructions from Austin by then."

He looked from man to man.

"Any questions?"

There were none.

"That is all. Be careful out there. I don't want to find anyone missing when we gather again."

As the men were breaking up, a humming sound could be heard in the distance.

Tom muttered, "What in heck?"

The sound got louder and louder, and sounded suspiciously like... a lawnmower, of all things.

All heads turned to Broadway Avenue, to the west of the courthouse.

And all were baffled when someone on a go-cart sped past them, barely visible in the moonlight, headed east at top speed.

Chapter 50

For the first time since he and Tom partnered up, Randy was working solo. They'd played bicycle leapfrog again on the way back to Randy's house, just as they had the evening before.

By the time they got back to Randy's apartment it was less than two hours before daybreak.

"I don't like breaking up the partnership," Randy suggested. "But we can get twice as much done, help twice as many people, if we split up. You work your neighborhood and I'll work mine."

"Agreed. But let me know when you want to go and get the horses. It'll be easier on you if we bike it there. We can leave the bike in the care of the stable master for the time being."

"Okay. Why don't you go check on your girlfriend and get some rest? Then come back here and pick me up in the early afternoon and we'll set out for the stables. That should get us back before sundown. We'll spend today working with the community and set out for the office together the next morning. Sound good to you?"

"Sounds good. I hope the major has some news by then that'll shed some light on what's happening."

They'd heard sporadic gunfire during the night from the steps of the federal building and during the long trip back home again.

Looters, they assumed, were being shot at by angry homeowners and shopkeepers.

Or maybe the riots had already started.

Traditionally during long blackouts, riots didn't start until the second night. Citizens were apt to give the power companies some leeway at first, trying their best to be patient while the power companies found the problems and fixed them.

By the second night, though, their patience usually wore thin. That was when the angriest of the citizens felt a need to let their anger be known. They did so by breaking store windows, setting fire to cars, and firing weapons into the air.

Doing such things never made things better, of course, other than to let a few of the more irresponsible feel better about themselves and their plight. It was nothing more than feeble minded jerks exerting their power and anger over the sound of mind, in the same way a bully on the playground likes to puff out his chest occasionally and yell obscenities.

Perhaps the riots were starting early because there was a general sense this was something more than a typical blackout.

In any event, since Randy had heard gunshots coming from the general direction of his apartment complex as he and Tom made their way from downtown, he worried. He worried about his neighbors and his friends.

He worried about what his city might turn into if somebody didn't fix this problem pronto.

In his complex, things were quiet. His neighbors apparently sensed that the safest place to be during a blackout was safely tucked in their own homes. Let the looters and rioters rule the city. Come out in the daylight hours, when the looters and rioters yielded once again to the decent people.

It was, in Randy's estimation, a prudent plan.

As Randy crawled into bed, intent on letting his weary body rest and his mind get some much needed sleep, a violent scene was playing out in the city around him.

The looters were indeed out. In great numbers. They were shattering windows in retail stores on every block of every commercial street. Those security guards who'd managed to make it to work, and the rare policeman who lived close enough to try to quell the chaos just stood by. They were outnumbered ten to one.

The United States' liberal gun policies worked well from some points of view, and spelled disaster by the accounts of others. From one respect, more than half the households in Lubbock had weapons. That made it easy for a family to cozy up inside their home, safe in the knowledge that anyone climbing in their windows to steal could be dealt with quickly and permanently.

On the other hand, the ease with which legal guns could be bought in America also meant that there was a glut of them. Many times the number available in other developed countries. The more guns there were, the more guns were stolen, then sold on the streets to gangs and hoods.

And looters.

So not only were the security guards and cops outnumbered ten to one, they could be fairly certain that at least some of those ten were armed. Most were probably convicted felons who had no desire to go back to jail. Or drug users who were desperate to get money for their next fix.

And then there were the opportunists. A blackout tends to bring out the worst of people. There's a certain element of looters who are law abiding citizens. They would never dream of pulling off a burglary under normal conditions. But during a blackout they have a lot of time to think while sitting in a darkened room staring at a blackened television set. They grow frustrated, angry at the power company. They start to seethe.

Some of them leave their homes out of curiosity, to see what's going on in the world around them. Some leave their homes because they can't sleep and there's nothing else to do.

They see the looting going on. Dozens of people just walking into the big box stores empty handed and exiting a minute later with a television set or a fistful of jewelry. And then they remember how much they hate the big box store. The lines are always too long and their cashiers are rude and their produce is always out of date.

Sometimes it'll occur to them that this may be their one and only chance to get even with the box store for all the times it's wronged them. Maybe get some restitution for that time that store clerk snarled at them.

And they join the mob.

On this particular night, every retail store in the city would be hit. Most of what would be taken wasn't essential to survival. Nobody wasted their time lugging out a case of water or canned goods. Instead they took televisions, CDs, laptop computers.

And it wouldn't dawn on any of them until long after the fact that their efforts were wasted. The risks they took were pointless.

Because every TV and computer and CD they took that particular night was absolutely worthless.

Chapter 51

By sunrise the city looked like it had been at siege for months.

The parking lots of every department store, every grocery store, and many smaller retail establishments were littered with merchandize. The sidewalks with broken glass. It looked like the morning after turmoil of a New Year's Eve party.

In short, it was a huge mess.

The looters were gone by now, having seen the sky start to lighten and decided it was time to vamoose. Or, having worn themselves out hours before from having to physically carry their loot home because their beat up old Chevys weren't working.

Many of the looters finally went to bed in the wee hours of the morning, gleeful that they'd been able to score and get away with it, and wondering how much money they could get for their booty.

Absolutely none. But none of them knew that yet.

Randy awoke just after noon, his aching body coaxing him to get up and take some aspirin.

The previous day and night he'd run several times farther than he was used to running, and his muscles were none too happy about it.

On Tom's bicycle, he'd used muscles he wasn't used to using. Then he overused them, and they were screaming at him too.

He slowly got out of bed and stumbled through his apartment, raising all the blinds to let the sunshine in. Then he made his way to the kitchen, opened the cabinet where he kept his medicine, and selected a bottle of Tylenol.

He almost opened the refrigerator for a cold bottle of water, then thought better of it. The less often he opened the door the longer the unit would remain cool on the inside. And the better the chance he'd be able to salvage some of the food.

Instead he pulled a warm bottle of Dasani from a case in the corner of the kitchen and used it to swallow the tablets.

It would take twenty minutes for the soreness and stiffness to go away. In the meantime, he moved gingerly as he got dressed for the day. He wanted a shower so much, but wanted to conserve the water in his hot water heater, in case he had to drink it at some point. A clean change of clothes would help, but not much. He felt like a walking, talking funk machine.

But it couldn't be avoided.

He turned on the gas stove. At least it still worked. He could cook some bacon and eggs before they went bad. He could heat some bottled water for coffee. The rest of his day might be absolutely terrible, but at least he'd start it out with a reasonably nice breakfast.

While his water was boiling he opened his front door and stepped out onto his stoop. The day was crisp and clear. The birds were singing and a light breeze cooled his face.

Under different circumstances he'd have thought he had a beautiful day ahead of him.

In any event, it was a good time for him to check out the situation in his neighborhood. Breakfast would wait a few more minutes. He went back to his kitchen and turned off the burner, then walked through his apartment complex to survey any damage the blackout had brought to it.

There were no visible signs of any looting or rioting. Apparently the looters had contained themselves to the commercial districts, which were infinitely safer than breaking into occupied homes. Randy was glad. He knew many of his neighbors and liked nearly all of them. He certainly wanted to see no harm come to them, and no assaults against their property.

He exited the west end of the complex and gazed out once again at Loop 289 and the sea of abandoned cars it held. Most of the hoods were down now, the people gone home. It looked almost calm now, as opposed to the angry and chaotic scene it had been the day before. It looked almost... serene.

And quiet. Oh, so quiet.

But the quiet didn't last long. From the north Randy's ears picked up what sounded at first like a tiny mosquito buzzing around his head. Then, as it grew louder, he realized it wasn't an insect at all. He cocked his head to the north in anticipation, and a few seconds later was treated to one of the most bizarre scenes he'd ever witnessed.

Speeding past him on the freeway, headed south, was a uniformed police officer driving a red go-cart with the number "94" painted on its side.

Crouched behind him, hanging onto the first officer's shoulders for dear life, was a second uniformed officer.

Randy wondered where they were going in such a hurry.

But it didn't matter. He had plenty to do on this particular day without worrying about cops on go-carts.

When he returned to his apartment he went a different route, this time passing by Mrs. Swenson's building.

He decided to knock on their door and offer to make them some breakfast, then offer to walk her and David back to his house, to make sure they made it there safely.

Mrs. Swenson was a woman who loved to chatter, and often when she got started it was hard to break away from her. David being there should help. Telling her he had to get the bacon started would as well.

As he drew closer and closer to the Swenson apartment it became more and more apparent something was wrong.

The screen on the storm door was ripped, as though someone had placed his hand on it to force the door open.

The front door was ajar.

Randy rapped on the door and called out, "Mrs. Swenson? David? Are you okay?"

No answer.

He intentionally rapped a little harder, causing the door to swing open a bit more.

He peeked into the darkened room, hand on his service weapon, as he called again.

"Mrs. Swenson? David? Are..."

He needn't finish the sentence. The two bodies he saw lying next to each other on the living room floor served to answer his query quite well.

David and his mother definitely *weren't* okay.

His weapon now in front of him, Randy called out, "Peace Officer, I'm coming in!" He cautiously went from room to room to clear the house.

No one else was there.

He was careful only to touch what he had to. He wished he had a pair of vinyl gloves to wear.

The apartment was very dimly lit, the draperies still drawn from the night before. The only light came from the sun streaming into the now wide-open door and between the drapes.

Randy carefully opened the drapes and raised the blinds to bathe the room in sunlight.

They'd been executed. They'd been on their knees, side by side, their hands bound behind them. They were killed with one shot apiece, to the backs of their heads, and had fallen forward onto their faces.

"But why?"

Randy didn't know it, but it was an answer he'd ask himself a thousand times. And as time went by and the years ticked away, he'd never learn the answer to his plaintive question. Why would anyone do this? Why?

He hoped they died quickly.

He said a quick prayer over their bodies and walked over to his car. He opened the trunk and took out a roll of yellow crime scene tape and a stapler, then went back and placed a big "X" across the doorway.

While he was securing the scene, Tom rode up on his bicycle.

"Whatcha doing, partner?"

"Double murder. An old woman and her grown son."

Tom could see the pain in Randy's eyes.

"Friends of yours?"

Then his history with Mrs. Swenson came out. And it explained the affection he had for her.

"Mrs. Swenson was my high school English teacher. She was like a second mom to me, almost."

Chapter 52

Less than a mile away from Randy's house, in a subdivision of upper middle class houses, Steve sat in front of a ham radio console. He was trying to raise his friend Tony in Fort Worth.

"Tony, this is Steve. You on?"

"Yeah, buddy. How are things your way?"

Steve cackled like an old witch.

"Place is going to hell in a hand basket. I guess we showed 'em after all, didn't we?"

"Yes, my friend, we did. Them bastards laughed at us. Called us crazy. Now it's just a matter of time before they come kissing our asses. Offering their apologies. Begging us to share what we got with them. But now's not the time to be cocky. Now's the time to be cautious. How's your blackout coming?"

"Good. I'll have the windows all painted and the shades all drawn by the end of the day. By tonight the inside of the house will be lit up like always. And from my front yard it'll look as dark and dreary as every other house on the street."

"And your front room?"

"Already took all the furniture out of it. It's as bare as a newborn baby. I hung the eviction notice last night around midnight, and during the daytime it'll look abandoned. Won't be any reason for looters to come looking in my house, no sirree. Nothing to see here, folks. Move right along now."

"Good boy."

"Say Tony, how's the situation to the east of you?"

To the "east" meant the metropolis of Dallas, Texas. Steve and Tony were careful never to reveal their locations when they talked on the ham radio. To do so would have alerted others in their area that they not only had working radios, but electricity to power them.

And those who had the ability to protect such things from the blackout would quite possibly have protected other things of value. That would have made them big targets.

It was an unwritten rule among "preppers." Share information with your friends to help each other out. But never, ever, give away your exact location. Not even to your friends. Because if your friends weren't as prepared as you were, they could someday become your enemies.

"I talked to another friend over that way this morning. He said all hell broke loose last night. Looters and gang activity mostly. They still haven't caught on that a can of soup is worth more than a high end TV set. They're stealing mostly electronics and carrying them all the way back to their neighborhoods. Then apparently the street gangs are meeting them there, saying, 'thank you for delivering my new TV to me,' and shooting the looters."

Steve laughed.

"Hell, let 'em take each other out. Darwinism at its finest. How you set for provisions?"

"Got enough for my group for about six months."

It was a lie. Another cardinal rule of prepping was not telling others exactly how much food, water and ammunition were in your stores. It could make them jealous enough to come looking.

"Yeah, me too."

The truth was, Tony had enough for his group of ten family members and friends for at least five to six years, depending on how many of them were killed in the chaos.

And Steve was flying solo. He claimed to have his own group of armed men and family members but he was all alone in the world. His whole family had pretty much written him off as crazy long before, and now had nothing to do with him. And that was fine by him.

And the six months of provisions? He had enough stashed to keep a single man alive for at least twenty years.

"Stay in touch, my friend. I need to get back to it."

During the daytime, the house at 5708 Ridgemont Drive in Lubbock would appear to be vacant. The large picture window next to the front door was unencumbered by draperies or shades. Anyone peering into it would see a completely empty room. The closet door and bathroom doors were both wide open and both similarly barren.

Posted on the window, for the benefit of curious neighbors, was an official looking letter from the First Bank of Fort Worth.

Across the top of the letter were the words "Eviction Notice," made out formally to Steve using his first, middle and last names.

It went on to say he had forty eight hours to vacate such property, as it was being foreclosed by the bank.

And it was dated three days before.

Nosy neighbors might wonder how old Steve had managed to move all his stuff and leave the neighborhood without anyone noticing.

But then again, it wouldn't be the first time someone got mired into debt and snuck away in the middle of the night to avoid the gazes of snooty neighbors.

Had one of the looters broken the front window and climbed through it, they'd have found the eviction was merely a ruse. On the other side of the empty front room, the house looked completely different. It was occupied and furnished and quite comfortable. It was also equipped with an elaborate set of blackout curtains and windows spray painted jet black from the inside to hide the fact that someone was living there.

Other than the empty front bedroom, Steve had the run of the full house during the day. The generator running all day long in the basement would help him maintain more or less the same lifestyle he'd always led, with some exceptions.

The television stations were down now, probably forever. But that was okay. For Steve had been prepping for years. He not only had over two thousand VHS tapes, each full of eight hours of evening television programing. But he also had ten VHS players, brand new and still in their boxes, which he'd bought for pennies on the dollar when their manufacturer stopped making them.

They were old school, sure. But who cared? Steve had no one to impress but himself. Everyone else be damned.

Cell phones, and telephones in general, was another thing he'd have to learn to live without. But it wasn't like he had a lot of friends to communicate with anyway. The few friends he did have would assume he ran away to someplace safe. If, that was, they even bothered to come and look for him.

It would take awhile to adjust to his new diet, which consisted of mostly dried goods. But he had fresh seeds and a place to plant them once planting season came around. He'd do okay. He'd survive until most of the world was dead. And someday, when it was safe enough to come out again, he'd be one of the very few who could rightfully declare themselves victors.

And he'd own a good piece of the city of Lubbock. Hell, for all he knew, he'd own most of Texas. For by that time, damn near everybody would be dead either by their own hand or somebody else's.

While he sat in his castle, eating baloney sandwiches and watching *Matlock* on television.

Chapter 53

They'd been saps. All of them. They thought he was crazy when he started talking about the end of the world as everyone knew it. They said he was a lunatic, and avoided him like the plague. Even his own family wouldn't have anything to do with him anymore. They said it was a damn shame, the way he squandered his savings and his pension and disability checks. On what, they asked. On dreams?

Steve checked his watch. He had two hours of daylight left. Two more hours before he'd retire to his secret basement for a peaceful night's rest and let the world collapse around him.

Time to do some work.

The last shipment of dry food that UPS had brought to his door had been two days before. Five cases of MREs. A twenty pound case of beef jerky. A twenty five pound bag of rice, a twenty five pound bag of lima beans and a twenty five pound bag of pinto beans.

He'd tossed them on a pile of similar items in his basement temporarily, until he had time to break them down. Now he had the time.

He turned the volume up on his MP-3 player until his earbuds vibrated within his ears. Patsy Cline singing *Crazy*. He laughed at how many people had used that term over the years to describe him. But he was right and they were all wrong. So who was the crazy one now?

He stepped past the bookcase full of books that was turned ninety degrees from an open doorway. Walked past the door, which was bolted securely to the back of the bookcase. Through the doorway and down the basement steps.

Down to the completed basement which covered over a thousand square feet. The exact footage as the first floor of the house above it.

He grabbed the bag of pinto beans and walked past the closed door of the generator room. A ten-thousand watt gas generator hummed softly inside, its sound dulled by a series of baffles and mufflers which made it as silent as a kitten's purr.

It was vented to the outside of the house through ductwork that Steve installed himself. Through the roof, so no one happening by would detect the smell of engine exhaust coming from the outer wall of the seemingly vacant house.

It was one of many secrets the walls in Steve's house contained. Secrets that no one, not even his family or closest friends, were aware of.

Up the stairs he went with the bag of beans over his shoulder. Back to the first floor, through his secret basement door. Then through the den and up to his second floor.

To the bedroom on the northeast corner of the house.

When he bought the house years before, his brother asked him why a single man would want or need a four bedroom house with a three car garage.

"I'm dating a woman with three kids," he'd said. "It's getting pretty serious and I think we may be married soon."

There was no woman. There were no kids. There certainly wasn't any impending marriage. Steve lied, as he'd done so many times since he'd become a prepper.

The truth was, Steve bought the house knowing it was going to be his base of operations for many years once solar storms sent electromagnetic pulses raining down on the earth.

He'd known for years that it was just a matter of time. Just a matter of time before the EMPs shorted out everything on earth that ran on electricity or electronics. The clues were there for anyone to pick up on. But nearly everybody ignored the clues, just as they'd ignored signs that Hitler was becoming a major threat in the 1930s. Just as they'd ignored the signs that the moon landing was a hoax. That Kennedy was shot by a team of Cuban assassins. That burning fossil fuels was destroying the environment.

The signs were all there. But they'd buried their heads in the sand and tried not to think about the possibility a big disaster was coming. It was just easier for them to convince themselves it wasn't.

That people like Steve were just nuts.

In the northeast bedroom he took the box of quart-sized zip-lock bags off the bed and pulled a few out. Then he used a box cutter to slice open the top of the bean bag and put it side, repeating a task he'd done at least a hundred times before.

One at a time, he filled the quart-sized zip-lock bags roughly half full. Then he zipped each bag closed, careful to remove as much of the excess air as he could.

They'd last for decades, even with extra air in the bags, as long as they were dry.

But they took up much less storage space with the air removed.

He emptied one box of zip-locks and part of another. And he used up over an hour of his remaining lifetime. But eventually he filled the last of the little plastic bags and tossed the empty bean bag to one side.

That was the tedious part. The next step would go a little quicker.

A home invader walking into the room would see nothing extraordinary about it. A single bed, a dresser, a closet full of children's clothing.

If the invader noticed anything unusual at all about the room, he might wonder about the kid's fascination with dinosaurs.

The bed was covered with stuffed brontosauruses, pterodactyls and t-rexes.

The walls were covered with posters displaying similar creatures. Some cartoonish, some scary. Some with dagger-like teeth dripping with blood.

And some with pink polka-dots, smiles on their faces and sailor hats on their heads.

Each of them, friendly and ferocious alike, shared a similar secret.

All of them covered holes, carefully cut into the sheetrock behind them, which contained a treasure-trove of survival supplies and provisions.

And they thought him crazy as a loon.

Chapter 54

Steve removed a large poster of Barney the Dinosaur hugging an armful of young fans with an oversized grin on his oversized purple face.

He placed the poster carefully aside, so as not to wrinkle it.

By taking the poster down from the west wall, he exposed a perfectly carved hole in the sheetrock just above his head, approximately fourteen inches wide and four inches high.

Then he prepared the zip-locked bags of beans by rolling each into a tube. He took a roll of brown packaging twine from the same dresser drawer which contained several addition boxes of zip-lock bags, and wrapped the twine tightly around the first rolled bag. He knotted it to keep it from coming unraveled, leaving the twine uncut. He prepared each additional zip-lock bag in the same manner, leaving about two feet of twine between each bag.

When he was done he had twenty one rolled bags, each containing a little over a pound of dried beans, each held to the others by a long continuous piece of heavy duty twine.

He took a small step ladder from the bedroom's closet and cozied it up against the wall beneath the hole. He was a rather diminutive man and needed the small ladder to comfortably complete the rest of his task. Of course, he could have carved the hole in the wall at his own eye level. But then the hollow space between the walls wouldn't have held as many provisions. And it was more likely to be discovered.

A looter leaning against the wall in this nondescript bedroom might have felt the hole behind one of the many posters in the room.

But not if the hole was way above his head.

He slowly eased the first of the zip-lock bags into the hole and let it work its way all the way to the floor between the walls. Then each successive bag in his string.

As he'd known from past experience, the twenty one bags fit nicely in the wall, as would many more.

Once done, he fastened the end of the twine to the wall just below the opening and held it in place with a flat thumbtack so it wouldn't drop into the hole. Then he replaced the poster to its original position and stepped back to admire his handiwork.

A looter who came into the room looking for valuables would likely rummage through the dresser drawers. He'd likely go through the closet, tossing things from the shelves inside onto the floor below.

He might even look between the mattresses, or beneath the small bed.

And he'd find absolutely nothing of value.

He'd likely leave the room frustrated, not knowing the treasure he'd left behind.

For the four walls between them held enough hidden food to keep a grown man alive for five years.

Yes, all four walls. For the summer after moving into the house, while still working a full time job, Steve had busied himself in the evenings and on weekends with a massive project.

One wall at a time, in each of the upstairs rooms, he'd carefully removed the sheetrock on the exterior walls and pulled out the insulation to hollow out the walls. Then he removed the electrical outlets on each exterior wall and disposed of them. He was careful to cap off the ends of the wiring left behind, to prevent fires, and when done he covered the exposed studs with a brand new sheet of sheetrock.

His three car garage looked like a construction site. The west bay had contained a waist-high pile of demolished sheetrock and ripped up pieces of wall insulation.

The east bay contained a stack of sheetrock, brought in discretely a few sheets at a time from a nearby Home Depot.

Each time he'd brought home more sheetrock, he'd purchased it just before the big orange home improvement store closed, then parked his pickup a few blocks from his house at a seldom-used city park.

Well after midnight on those nights he'd retrieved the pickup and brought it home, backing into the center bay of his darkened garage.

Getting rid of the material was a little bit easier, since the windows of his Ford Explorer were heavily tinted.

He merely crammed the back of the vehicle full of the waste and trucked it to the local dump ground when the pile became unmanageable. Always on an extended lunch hour on a weekday, when he was unlikely to run into anyone he knew along the way.

All those saps were still working for the man and thinking they were getting somewhere.

Steve, the smartest man he knew, would survive all of them. For while they were slaving away for a paycheck, Steve was preparing for Armageddon.

The wall replacement project had taken four months, and had been a major pain in the ass. But it was worth it. It doubled the amount of his hidden storage upstairs, and would extend his food stores by many years.

The following summer he did the same thing to the downstairs.

There were some drawbacks, of course. Serious ones, which made Steve wonder occasionally whether it was all worth it.

The first problem was the mess. A very fine coating of gypsum power covered everything in the house, and was difficult to clean. The same powder got into the carpet and turned it pure white. It took almost a full year of constant vacuuming and dusting to return the renovated house to its original condition.

But once it was clean the house had become the perfect hiding place.

The other major drawback to Steve's hidden stores was that dried beans, rice, and elbow macaroni didn't insulate his outer walls quite as well as R-19 fiberglass insulation.

His heating bills skyrocketed during the winter months. His cooling bills did the same in the summer.

But he foresaw that and accepted it. His solution was merely to shut the vents in the upstairs ceilings and close the rooms off. Since the ductwork was no longer needed to move air, the two hundred feet of insulated ductwork in the attic was the perfect hiding place for four hundred pounds of boxed spaghetti noodles.

He turned off all the lights on both floors of his house just before the sun went down and headed for the basement steps. Once inside, he grabbed the handle on the back of the basement door. The door, and the bookcase full of books attached to it, closed behind him.

Getting the bookcase perfectly mounted to the basement door took quite a bit of adjusting. It was one of the project's bigger pains in Steve's ass. But it was worth it. The bottom of the bookcase cleared the top of the carpet by less than a sixteenth of an inch. Not enough to disturb it at all. Not enough to make anyone question what had been dragged across the carpet directly in front of the bookcase and look at it more closely.

To anyone standing in front of the bookcase, or anywhere else in the room, it was merely a bookcase pushed against a wall.

And since very few of the other homes in the neighborhood had basements, there was no reason to suspect this house had one either.

On the other side of the bookcase and door, on the landing where eighteen steps led to the basement below, Steve fastened two slide bolts that held the door securely in place.

Even if someone on the outside suspected there was more to meet the eye, his shaking of the bookcase would yield or reveal nothing. It wouldn't budge at all.

And that wouldn't be a surprise at all. Not for a solid oak bookcase full of heavy books.

It was but one perfect ruse in a sea of ruses.

Steve had done his job well.

The generator had run for approximately four hours that day, and had charged his wall-sized bank of storage batteries completely.

It was those batteries which would power his electrical needs until he emerged from his basement hiding place the next day.

He switched the generator power selection switch from "Program" to "Off" and popped a bag of microwave popcorn in to cook. Then he put in an old John Wayne movie to watch.

Let the rest of the world disintegrate into chaos. He didn't care.

It was nothing but a minor inconvenience to Steve.

Chapter 55

Randy knocked on the door of another neighbor, a Lubbock Police homicide detective, and walked with him over to the apartment where he'd discovered the two bodies.

"Thanks for securing the scene," the detective told him. "I don't know when we'll be able to recover the bodies. Or how we'll move them. Or where. But I'll take this one off your hands so you can attend to other things."

Attend to other things he did.

It was easier to cover ground once he and Tom were on horseback. They spent the better part of two days helping reunite family members, soothing frayed nerves and reassuring citizens that the way to keep everyone safe was to stay calm and to work together.

Randy and Tom suspected that the Federal Reserve had collapsed and that the dollar was now worthless. But in absence of any confirmation of that, they were accepting money from their friends and neighbors in exchange for bottled water from a nearby supermarket.

The supermarket had a pharmacy inside, and looters had smashed several of its front windows on the first night of the blackout, looking for drugs.

The store was now abandoned, its employees having no way to get to work and no way to ring up sales if they had made it in. Randy was able to fashion an oversized set of saddlebags from two military deployment bags, each side capable of carrying two cases of drinking water.

He was accepting five dollar bills from the citizens, which he dutifully placed in the center of the desk of the supermarket manager. One five dollar bill for every case of water he took out of the store.

He couldn't help but wonder how long the stack of bills would sit there gathering dust before someone happened in and found them.

At one point he was delivering water to a woman three streets from his own when she went into labor.

With no formal training other than emergency first aid, he found himself working alongside a nurse who appeared from nowhere and helped deliver the baby. A little boy, who appeared healthy despite the rather austere conditions.

He hoped there were no complications after he left, but made a mental note to stop by in a few days to check in on mother and child.

As they'd been instructed by Major Shultz, Randy and Tom reported for duty at high noon the third day of the blackout.

They found that "high noon," when judged from the position of the sun, was highly subjective. They got there when they thought the sun was at its highest point, but Randy's wind-up watch was still keeping perfect time. And it said 11:15.

The last Ranger to arrive did so a little after one p.m., and he thought he was early.

It turned out that all ten Rangers present had a different interpretation of "high noon."

They needed a more reliable way of coordinating their meetings, for Randy was the exception to the rule. He still had a watch which worked. Everyone else had cast aside wind-up watches years before and gone with more modern timepieces. And none of them worked anymore.

While half the Rangers milled about on the steps of the federal building, Major Shultz ran upstairs to get something from his office and handed it to Randy.

"What's this, sir?"

"It's a purchase order and draft. After you leave here today, your first order of business is to visit the local

Walmart. It's probably been broken into like all the other retail stores. Go to their jewelry department and see if you can find a dozen wind-up watches, similar to the one you have. Use your math skills to figure up a total and write it in the blank. Then leave this on one of the cash registers. Bring the watches to our next meeting in two days. Got it?"

"Yes, sir."

When the last Ranger showed, the major started his meeting.

"We're going to do this down here on the steps, boys, because the offices are dark and stifling. I was hoping the building's generator survived and we could get the power restored, but that's not the case.

"We haven't been able to get ahold of Austin, so we're still flying blind. Our mission will continue to be helping the citizens of Lubbock as best we can until we get our marching orders from Ranger HQ.

"However, I can at least shed some light on what we're dealing with.

"I've been talking with the local authorities. Some of them have been in touch with the scientists and professors at Texas Tech University. The earth has been zapped by a massive electromagnetic pulse."

Several of the Rangers looked at each other, puzzled. One murmured, "Electrowhat what?"

"Electromagnetic pulse. It's generated on the surface of the sun during extremely active solar storm activity. An EMP is essentially an arc that reaches the earth. It's similar to the little arc of electricity that goes from your fingers to your doorknob after you've dragged your feet through the carpet. Only this one is a lot more powerful. And it doesn't hurt humans. It does its damage to machines."

"Major, are you saying that electricity from the sun shorted everything out?"

"Yes. In simple terms, yes."

"Well, how long does it last?"

"Nobody seems to know. The vehicles and machines that were shorted out have to be rebuilt. The problem is, it'll take massive quantities of materials and labor to make everything needed to rebuild everything. And you can't run the factories without the machines. And you can't power the machines without electricity. And you can't fix things without the materials the factories produce.

"So it's kind of a Catch 22 situation. And nobody knows how long to get things back to the way they were. Some of the more optimistic scientists said a decade or two. Some of the more pessimistic ones said never. At least not in our lifetimes."

At that moment a uniformed cop on a go-cart sped past the on his way to police headquarters.

One of the Rangers asked, "What is it with those damn go-carts? That's about the tenth one I've seen in the last two days."

The major shook his head sadly.

"The LPD has forty of the go-carts, but they're using them for themselves. Can't say I blame them. One of their retired officers owns a go-cart track just outside the city limits and loaned them to the city of Lubbock. Each of their patrolmen was issued a go-cart and a section of water hose five feet long."

"What's the hose for?"

"The fuel tanks on those things are pretty small. They can go about five or six miles to a tank. Then they have to stop and siphon gas from an abandoned car to get going again."

"That sucks."

"Yeah, but at least they don't have to let their vehicles graze or clean up their poop like we do."

"But Major Shultz, how come those things run but cars don't?"

"Because cars have batteries and electronic ignitions that were shorted out. The engines on the go-carts start with a pull-cord, like a lawnmower. They don't have batteries or ignitions."

"Can I ask one of the cops if he'll trade me his go-cart for my horse?"

"You may not. We're not going to ride around on go-carts and have the citizens of Lubbock point at us and laugh."

"The Lubbock cops do."

"They're not Rangers."

Chapter 56

Steve finished hiding another twenty five pound bag of beans and a fifty pound of rice in a wall in the southwest bedroom.

It gave him a headache.

He walked down to his basement sanctuary and popped a couple ibuprofen tablets. Then he sat at his desk and pulled out a ledger.

Steve was an immaculate records-keeper. The people he once worked with thought him to be OCD, but he wasn't. In most respects he was a slob. He didn't care whether his dishes got done every night and didn't care which side of his plate the silverware went on. Or how carefully the magazines were arranged on the coffee table.

But he'd always had a head for mathematics and an unhealthy obsession with numbers. And when it came down to adding or subtracting numbers, or doing any math project for that matter, he insisted on doing it right.

Even to the point of going back to triple check and quadruple check his work.

He saw his running inventory in the same light. He kept meticulous records of every bag of lima beans he crammed into which wall. Every one of the thousands of lightweight packages of Ramen noodles he stuffed into his attic. Every can of tuna and spam he shoved into hollowed out mattresses. Every one of the four hundred cases of bottled water which lined the outer walls of his basement, from floor to ceiling.

And he checked and rechecked his numbers constantly. He didn't want to run out of anything because he failed to plan properly.

He watched an old movie while he waited for his headache to subside.

The Last Man on Earth, with Vincent Price.

Very fitting.

The movie ended and he pulled out a dog-eared copy of Charlie Bennett's *Preparing for Armageddon on a Budget.*

The prepper's bible.

That night he'd be sneaking outside to put inch and a half wood screws into his fence to keep out looters and the curious. He'd thought he had all his bases covered, until he found the book at a garage sale. Now he referred to it almost every day for tips and advice.

There was a knock on the front door.

He could barely hear it, and only because his desk was at the bottom of the basement steps.

The knock grew louder.

Steve smiled.

He put his book aside and walked up the steps.

Only one man he knew of would ignore the eviction notice on the front window and knock on the door of a seemingly vacant house.

He looked out the peephole, just to verify his suspicions.

This time a smile wasn't enough. He outright chuckled.

He opened the door and smiled at the man standing on the other side.

It was none other than Major John Shultz, of the Texas Rangers.

Steve stepped to one side so that the major could enter and said, "I've been expecting you."

****

Thank you for reading
RANGER, Book 1
A Humble Beginning

Please enjoy this preview of
RANGER, Book 2:
A Whole New World

A Whole New World will be available worldwide in August, 2016

****

He'd seen more than his share of death, lost more than his share of friends. But this was somehow different.

He'd felt a lot of guilt when his parents died. He'd felt he could have made their last years easier, more pleasant, if only he'd known. But there was nothing he could have done to save either of them. He knew that and accepted it.

With Tom it was different.

With Tom, if he'd done things differently he might have been there. He might have prevented his partner's death.

Now he was alone again. He'd failed on his efforts thus far to find Sarah. The vision of her still haunted him when he closed his eyes each night. But perhaps he wasn't meant to find her. Perhaps it was his destiny to have only those fleeting memories of her.

His family was gone. The one girl in the whole of Lubbock he wanted to find and protect was out there somewhere, but he knew not where.

And now his partner was gone as well.

He couldn't bring back his family. He couldn't find his Sarah.

But he could find the man who gunned down Tom.

He looked down at the crude marker he'd made with a black marks-a-lot and a paving brick.

TOM COHEN
A Good Man. A Godly Man. A Ranger.
Rest in Peace, My Friend

It embarrassed him that he couldn't remember Tom's birthday.

But it didn't matter much. The marker said enough.

"I'm sorry I couldn't save you, buddy. But I promise that as long as it takes, I'll avenge you."

****

If you enjoyed
RANGER, Book 1
A Humble Beginning

You might also enjoy
RED: The Adventure Begins

Available now at Amazon.com and Barnes and Noble Booksellers.

Here's a preview...

****

Red had a worried look on her face.

And Red never worried about anything.

"Dad, I don't like this. This isn't just a typical blackout. This is something worse. Much worse."

"Now, honey, don't jump to conclusions. It's only been a little more than a day. We've had blackouts that lasted longer than this before.

"Look at it like an unearned vacation. We didn't ask for it, but it's here. Let's take a day off and go fishing. Heck, we can't do anything here anyway."

But Red was adamant.

"No, Dad. You aren't listening. Haven't you noticed we haven't had any traffic since the power went out? I mean, *none*. In a day and a half we haven't had a single car roll into town. You know why? Because the cars are all dead, that's why.

"Bonnie and I rode up to the highway this morning. I wanted to see if I could find which transformer blew, and whether they had a crew out there replacing it.

"What I found instead were abandoned cars, as far as the eye could see, in either direction. Many of them had their hoods up, like their owners had been trying to get them running again.

"There are people up on the highway just wandering around, not knowing what to do. People sleeping in their cars. People in shock.

"Dad, what in the world could possibly cause all the cars to stop working at precisely the same time all the power went out?"

Her father's face suddenly turned ashen.

He stumbled over his words.

"A nuclear blast at high altitude could have caused it. But only a few countries have the capability of doing that. And they have no reason to. It would harm them as much as us.

"There's only one other thing I know of that could cause such chaos."

He didn't want to go on.

But she needed to know.

"One of the things pilots study is the affect the other planets and sun can have on our own planet. How their gravitational pulls can affect our compasses and such.

There's a phenomenon that can occur during a massive solar storm. If the storm is large enough, it can send electromagnetic pulses toward the earth. Those pulses can short out anything that runs on electrical power."

"Dad, please tell me it's just temporary. That things will start working again once the solar storm has passed."

"No, honey. I'm sorry. If that's what's caused this, then it's permanent."

He held her close before finishing.

"And we're all doomed."

****

If you enjoyed
RANGER, Book 1
A Humble Beginning

You might also enjoy
FINAL DAWN

Available now at Amazon.com and Barnes and Noble Booksellers.

****

What would you do if you finally found the love of your life, and were making plans to spend eternity together - and then found out that eternity was only two years? Mark is a romantic and carefree young engineer, and a bit of a cornball. His beloved Hannah is a beautiful scientist. Pragmatic, intelligent and analytical, she longs for the family she never had, and a change from her horrific childhood. Mark offers that change, and her life is finally complete.

Then Hannah discovers that mankind is doomed. Suddenly their lives become a mad scramble, to find a way to save themselves and everyone they love.

An excerpt from FINAL DAWN:

Sometimes the gods of fate smile upon you, and bestow on you a treasure of such magnitude, such wonder, that you pinch yourself over and over until you finally believe it's really real.

And sometimes those same gods bestow upon you a bowl of smelly, steaming crap.

They seldom do both within the same week.

Mark Snyder finished the breaker box tie in just before losing his daylight. He'd been working in an empty house for days, all alone in his thoughts. He hated jobs like this. No one to talk to, no other voices to listen to, other than the ones in his head. The house was only about eighty percent complete. Not far enough along yet to have power.

The electricians were supposed to button everything up by the end of the week. And yes, he could have waited until then to start installing the security system. But he had several other jobs going on at once, and he was trying to maintain his good reputation for coming in on time. So while most people would have taken Sunday off to watch the ball game and relax, he was here instead installing security cameras.

He'd come back on Saturday and check all the cameras to make sure they were working, then install the operations console.

But for now, he'd done everything he could do without electricity. He loaded his tools back into his Explorer and headed home. Enough is enough.

Mark picked up his cell and called Hannah.

"Hey, Babe. I'm on my way. Is the game still on?"

"Hi, honey," she said. "No, it's over, but you'll be proud of me. I recorded it for you so you can watch it when you get home. The Cowboys lost at the last second when Washington kicked a field goal."

Mark winced and bit his lip. He resisted the urge to tell her it's not so much fun watching a close game when you know how it turns out.

Instead, he praised her. Because after all, she was the light of his life and the best thing that ever happened to him.

"Well, thank you, my love." He said. "Are you trying to out-sweet me again?"

Hannah replied "Nope. Not trying. I won that contest a long time ago. I just wanted to show you how much I love you."

She went on. "If you want some beer you'll have to stop and get some. Bryan came by to watch the game with you. I told him you were working and he asked if we had some beer. I told him to check the fridge. He took all we had and left. Said if we weren't going to watch the game, then we wouldn't need it. He said he'd take it to someone who had the game on.

"How did you manage to grow up with him without ever killing him?"

Mark laughed. "Because he was the baby of the family and Mom always took his side. If I had killed him she'd have grounded me for at least a week, maybe two. But I thought about it many times."

He made a mental note to find a way to get back at his brother. And yes, he'd have to stop for beer. The last hour of the job tonight, the only thing that kept him going was the thought of downing a cold Corona or two.

Mark walked into the Exxon convenience store and waved at Joe Kenney, the assistant manager.

Mark shouted across the store as he pulled a six-pack of Corona from the cooler. "Hey, Joe! All that I have are these, to remember you."

A couple of the other customers gave Mark the strangest look. A "better stay away from this guy" kind of look.

Joe yelled back from behind the counter, where he was inventorying cigarettes. "Jim Croce. Photographs and Memories."

They'd known each other since high school, where Joe was one of the coolest guys Mark knew. Joe knew everything about music from the good old days. The music from the 60s and 70s. Back when music was good, and you could understand the lyrics. And every other word wasn't profane.

They'd played this game almost as long as they'd been friends. Mark would find an obscure song lyric and try to stump Joe. But he seldom succeeded. Joe played five instruments, and had been in various garage bands since he was ten. Music was pretty much his life. At least when he wasn't at Exxon counting cigarettes.

The line was a lot longer than usual. A rolling marquee above the cash register said the Powerball jackpot was at $310 million. Mark let out a slow whistle. That was a good chunk of change.

He seldom played the lottery himself, but Hannah did all the time. Poor sweet thing. She'd been stuck at home with the flu for the last week and hadn't been able to get out. But he knew she'd have gotten herself a ticket if she hadn't been sick.

So as a last-second lark, he told the clerk to throw in a quick pick for the lottery, cash option, and paid two extra bucks. It was worth two dollars to make Hannah smile that beautiful smile. And it was the least he could do for her, for thinking enough to record the game for him.

But Mark forgot to give her the ticket. Forgot to even take it into the house. He laid it on the passenger seat of his Explorer and it sailed down to the floorboard when a dog ran in front of him and he had to hit the brakes hard. And he pulled into the driveway, took his beer and watched the game, and never gave it another thought.

On Thursday, Mark was doing a sales pitch to a banker who was worried because his neighbor three doors down had been a recent victim of a home invasion. The banker's community was gated and a private security company made their rounds occasionally, but none of that had stopped the brazen thieves from posing as utility workers.

In broad daylight, they knocked on his neighbor's door, and flashed fake IDs to gain access to the back yard "to check the power lines." From there, they cut the phone cable, kicked in the back door, and tied up the occupants before leisurely looting the place of all its valuables. They even stopped long enough to make themselves a sandwich before leaving.

Thievery, it seems, works up one's appetite.

The banker decided he needed a better security system, and Mark was trying to convince him that he was the man for the job.

Mark's cell phone went off. A little bird whistling "I've Got Sunshine" told him he had a text message from Hannah. He hit the mute button and went on with his presentation.

Half an hour later he'd sealed the deal and was returning to his Explorer when he remembered the text. It said "Call me ASAP."

Oops.

But luckily Hannah wasn't mad. She was way too excited.

"Did you hear about Joe's store?" she asked him.

He answered with a bit of apprehension. "No. Did they get robbed again? Is he okay?"

"Oh, yeah, I'd say so! I heard on the news that they sold the winning ticket to the Powerball drawing. Somebody won over two hundred million dollars after taxes. And it's somebody that lives right here in San Angelo. Wouldn't it be cool if it's somebody we know?"

"Baby, hold on a minute."

Mark put the phone down and took out his wallet. The ticket he had purchased on Sunday night wasn't there. Crap! Did he leave it on the counter at the store? Did some cretin come up behind him and pick it up?

He instinctively felt his pants pockets, even though he knew he wasn't wearing the same jeans he had on Sunday night.

Then, on the floorboard of the passenger side of his ride, he saw a lonely piece of paper. And he remembered that damn dog.

He picked up the ticket, then the phone.

"Honey, don't freak out," he said. "But I bought you a ticket on Sunday night and forgot to give it to you. Would you go on line and see what the winning numbers are and read them to me?"

The next thirty seconds lasted twenty years.

Hannah came back on the line and said "Okay, here goes. 13, 25, 26, 44, 57, and the Powerball is 18."

Mark's chest actually started to hurt, and he felt faint. In his mind's eye, he saw Redd Foxx playing Fred Sanford, holding his chest and saying "This is it. It's the big one..."

But Mark wasn't having a heart attack. Mark was experiencing what it felt to find out that you were suddenly a multi-millionaire.

Hannah didn't believe him, of course. She thought he was playing one of his dumb practical jokes. She met him at the door as he walked in and presented her the ticket as a new father might present his first born to a hospital nursery visitor.

"Be careful," he said. "Don't damage it or tear it or sneeze on it."

The next day was Friday, and Hannah insisted on getting up and going to work. Even though she only got an hour's worth of sleep. Mark stayed behind in bed, telling her just to call in and say "Go to hell, you bastards. I'm rich!"

But Hannah was a scientist and an honorable one at that. She was above doing such a thing. She'd wait until her boss pissed her off. Then she'd tell the bastards to go to hell.

When they parted that morning, both of them were on cloud nine. They'd spent most of the night talking about all the great things they'd do with their new fortune. They laughed when they thought of sour old Reverend Samuels, and how he might actually crack a smile when they presented him with a tithe check for ten percent of their winnings.

They talked about which European countries they'd visit first, and even considered buying their own Caribbean Island.

Yes, when they parted that morning, neither had a care in the world.

What a difference a day makes.

****

Please enjoy this preview of
COUNTDOWN TO ARMAGEDDON.

COUNTDOWN TO ARMAGEDDON
**is available now at Barnes and Noble.com and
Amazon.com**

****

Scott Harter wasn't special by anybody's standards. He wasn't a handsome guy at all. He wasn't dumb, but he'd never win a Nobel Prize either. He had no hidden talents, although he fancied himself a fairly good karaoke singer.

His friends didn't necessarily share that opinion, but what did they know?

No, if those friends were tasked to choose one word to describe Scott Harter, that word might well be "average."

If Scott excelled at one thing, it was that he was a very good businessman. And he was also a lot luckier than most.

And it was that combination – his penchant for making a buck, and being lucky, that led him here on this day to the Guerra Public Library on the west side of San Antonio.

To research what he believed was the pending collapse of mankind.

Twenty three years earlier, Scott had done two things that would change his life forever. Even back then, he was just an average Joe. He'd had plans to become a doctor, but his average grades weren't cutting it. So he dropped out of college halfway through his junior year.

He'd have loved to have married a beauty queen, but his average looks certainly did nothing to attract any. Neither did his average amount of charm. So instead he started dating Linda Amparano, who was a sweet girl but somewhat average herself. They seemed to make a perfect, if slightly vanilla, couple.

The second thing Scott did that year was buy a dilapidated self-storage unit on the north side of San Antonio. It was one of those places where people rent lockers to store their things when their garages have run out of space. Or their kids go off to college. Or when they just accumulate so many things that they've run out of room to put them all.

Pat, the guy who sold the property to Scott, was a friendly enough sort, but not a businessman at all. He didn't understand some of the basic principles of running such an operation.

Not that Scott was an expert. At least back then he wasn't.

But even back then, Scott knew the value of curb appeal, and that a fresh paint job and a few repairs could attract a few more customers. And a few more customers would help supply money for advertising, and special offers, and long-term lease discounts. No brainers, actually.

So by the end of that year, two things happened. Scott had turned around the business and turned it into a money-making operation. And he married Linda.

The pair said their vows on December 17th of that year. It was bitterly cold that day. The coldest December 17th on record for that part of Texas.

If the cold was an omen, though, neither of them saw it. If either of them had, and had gotten cold feet, their lives would be so much different today.

But they just laughed it off, as young couples in love are wont to do. And they went ahead with their nuptials and started their lives together and never looked back at that cold day in December when they ran headlong into a marriage that shouldn't have happened.

The marriage lasted nine years. It produced two great sons, so there was that. And Scott and Linda remained friends. That was something else. So there was a good legacy, of sorts, left behind by their mistake that cold December day.

Scott adored his boys. There was Jordan, his oldest, who was intelligent and talented and a bit of a goofball. And there was Zachary, who Scott was convinced would someday become a scientist or a highly successful engineer. Zach was always taking things apart and making other things with them. His curious mind never stopped working, and he loved exploring new things and new ideas. Zach was sweeter than a bucket of molasses. He was everybody's best friend.

Yes, Scott was lucky as a father. No problems with his boys at all.

He was also lucky in that he lived in Texas at the time of the divorce. Texas wasn't an alimony state. So he wasn't saddled with monster alimony payments like his brother in Atlanta was. His brother Mike was divorced the same year as Scott, and was ordered by the court to pay forty percent of his before-tax income to a wife who had cheated on him multiple times.

No, Scott had no such problem. He paid child support, of course, and was always on time with it. And he doted on his boys and bought them nice things.

But since he didn't have to pay alimony, he was able to take that money instead and use it to build his business.

After the first storage facility was turning a healthy profit, he was able to buy a second. Then a third. And with each one he followed the same business model. He'd do some cosmetic improvements to attract a few more customers. Then he'd turn that additional income into air time on the local radio station, or ads in the local paper. Getting the word out drew more customers, which in turn would supply more money for special deals and discounts. Which would provide more money for another new facility.

It was a business model that had served him well.

And now, twenty three years later, Scott Harter owned a chain of thirty one storage facilities spread throughout San Antonio and nearby Houston.

So even though he wasn't as handsome as a movie star, and would never be a candidate to join Mensa, he was doing all right. And that was good enough for him.

Linda had remarried within a year. The marriage only lasted two years and was full of problems. She waited a bit longer to marry her third husband, and the third time seemed to be the charm for her. The third husband, Tony, was a good man, who treated Linda and the boys well. At least it appeared that way to Tony. He didn't know that since their divorce, Linda had gotten very good at putting on airs and keeping secrets. Keeping the ugly truth from Scott made it easier for Scott and Tony to be casual friends. Scott eventually found out that Tony was a con man and a user, who'd taken Linda for pretty much everything she had.

It was Scott who helped her get back on her feet. She banished Tony from her life, and swore off marriage forever.

From that point on, Linda chose a life less complicated. A life with an endless stream of boyfriends who didn't provide a sense of stability. But they were a lot easier to get rid of when they didn't work out.

Their boys had been brought up in a stable environment, which meant they were well behaved and relatively problem free. Neither of them ever got into drugs, or ran away from home. Neither of them had gone to jail, or left a string of broken hearts. Both of them were good kids, who had bright futures ahead of them. Or so they thought. Actually, there were problems ahead, which none of them knew about, but which their father would soon discover.

Yes, all in all, Scott was a lucky man, despite his being just an average guy. And he was living a pretty comfortable life.

That was about to change.

CPSIA information can be obtained
at www.ICGtesting.com
Printed in the USA
LVHW111314230420
654315LV00003B/628